Turn That Floozy Series

Vengeance Is Mine

ILAYA D. BROWN

Copyright © 2015 Ilaya D. Brown
All rights reserved.
ISBN 10: 1522967524
ISBN 13: 978-15229677521

DEDICATION

Giving honor to God, and all His splendor.

My daughter, who is the driving force of my motivation today.

CHAPTER TWENTY

The sweetest melody one can hear is the music of heaven. Living water flowing though the city where lights illuminate so brightly you can hardly see. The music like a river of voices singing, "Worthy is the Lamb that was slain." Instruments of a million strings playing in such a heavenly way, unlike anything heard before on earth. Blissful and peaceful are the only words to describe the feeling. The still, small voice comes to Natasha, saying, "Not yet daughter, not yet."

Natasha awakens to more familiar voices. They do not possess the same level of peace and comfort but they make her happy. Her mother is talking to Janet, who is close to her speaking in Spanish.

"You have been on that phone since ya got here. I do not want my daughter waking up from a coma speaking Spanish. Nathanel, tell her to get off tha phone right now."

"Mrs. Billingsworth, Natasha is used to me speaking Spanish. If anything, she will wake telling me to shut up. I have to make sure they cancel all my shows. Thank God it was a short tour, otherwise Nathanel would have to take care of me," replies Janet as she draws her face closer to his and their noses touch affectionately.

"Okay, you two," Michelle says to break their embrace, "Nathanel, your mother and brother are going to take shift in a few minutes, so let's prepare to clear out. We have to check on Jeffery. He is stable but critical from the gunshot. Ashley cleaned Nat's place for me and I need to tell her thank you. Get off that phone and come on here!"

Natasha can hear movement but she realizes no one knows she is awake. She feels trapped and everything feels heavy. If Natasha were to have a breakdown internally right now, no one would be able to detect it. A nurse enters the room and checks her stats. She must be thinking out loud when she says, "I am sorry this happened to you, honey. Your baby is alive and well in you, in spite of your three broken ribs and punctured lung. They will take time to heal. We are working hard to keep Jeffery alive. We know you didn't mean to shoot him, but he is getting better though he still has his good days and his bad days. Now, all we can do is wait and make sure everything heals properly. The rest of the family is on the way up to switch shifts. I keep telling you all these things so you won't be totally left out when you wake up."

Suddenly, a warm feeling comes over Natasha's entire body. It feels like fire is shut up in her bones. The only thing Natasha can do in reaction to this comforting heat is shout, "Jesus!" The machines around her start making noises and she can hear the still, small voice say, "He whom the Son sets free is free indeed."

The nurse, startled, drops everything in her hand. She yells down the hall for the doctor and extra help. Natasha can hear the clacking of stilettos and what sounds like a herd of buffalo. Her family had doubled back when they heard the nurse shout and they beat the staff to the room. The nurse uses her body to hold them off.

Doctor Milton arrives and pleas, "Let me through, please, it is critical that I see her before you can enter." The small mob parts way so that the doctor can take a look at Natasha.

The road to recovery is greater than she knows, but Natasha has the feeling of renewal and the will to push forward. She remembers most of the events that had been spoken of around her. The feeling that she has only been taking a power nap is awkward, but so is her shambled life at this point.

CHAPTER TWENTY-ONE

Doctor Milton looks like a mirage to Natasha due to her blurry vision. He shines a small light into her eyes to check her pupils. She winces in reaction and turns away.

"That is bright," Natasha informs.

"I know; I have to make sure everything is okay. I'm going to apply a little pressure to your abdomen to check your ribs and the baby's growth."

"Baby's growth? I do not understand. I am not pregnant," informs Natasha. She remembers the nurse telling her the baby was okay. It seems easier to be in denial than to accept her current reality further.

Doctor Milton pretends he does not hear her and uses his stethoscope to check her lungs. When he gently presses his hand against her eighth through tenth ribs, she sucks a large amount of air in through her teeth to keep from punching the doctor with her left hand.

"Obviously, there is something wrong and a definite mix-up. Your nurse said I had three broken ribs and you were able to save the baby. I can tell which ribs are broken from where you just touched me, but there is no way I can be pregnant! Oh, God. Am I the one who shot Jeffery or was it Little Bruce who kicked my ass? I do not remember Jeffery coming to my apartment. He was not even there. Could someone tell me something, now?"

Doctor Milton stands over Natasha when he finishes her examination and informs her, "You are at Lenox Hill Hospital and you have been in a coma for a month. It is Wednesday, November twelve. We have X-rays and scans done bi-weekly to monitor the healing process of your lung and the breaks. We drained the lung and the puncture has closed completely. The scar tissue has decreased and the bruising has gone down significantly. All is healing well. You are, in fact, five months pregnant. Your next ultrasound is scheduled for tomorrow morning. You will be envied by many, because you are not showing but as if you were only three months. Did you have any symptoms of morning sickness, or any butterflies in your stomach?"

"I only got butterflies when I saw Jeff. I hardly get sick, which explains my surprise at this big announcement, Doc."

Natasha plops her head on her pillow and lets out a long sigh. Tears begin to roll down her face. Her family and the nurse who had informed her of the current situation, are standing at the door.

Everyone is speechless, because there is much to discuss but too much to talk about for someone who has been asleep for a month. Doctor Milton breaks the silence with details of her recovery, saying, "Your ribs have bonded back together beautifully, but it will be another month before you will be one hundred percent; however, you should be aware that the baby's growth will cause you much pain in recovery. Everything looks to be fine. There will be few complications from here on out. We are going to keep you in tight gowns to maintain your posture and the healing process. Do you have any other questions for me?"

Natasha takes her left hand and rubs her stomach and asks before she knows it, "How soon could we schedule an abortion?"

Her family begins a rebuttal immediately, but no one can make out what they are saying. Tessa and Bryant Junior had arrived in time to hear the doctor inform Natasha of the situation. Janet, Nathanel, and Michelle stand behind the doctor. Janet has her hands clasped together and is praying in Spanish. Michelle is standing with her hands on her chest and tears streaming down her face.

Her brothers keep their faces stern, just as Bryant would have, but Tessa — being the firecracker she is — blurts out, "Doc, she just woke up. Give her enough time to take in all the information. You can give her the answer after the ultrasound tomorrow. You have been marvelous in orchestrating her recovery. I thank God for you, but if you will, could you leave? And the nurse, too."

As the doctor and the nurse exit the room Natasha commands her family, "Could all of you follow? I am not asking. I am telling you."

Her smug attitude gets under Michelle's skin for the last time. She begins saying through clenched teeth, "Listen here, you ungrateful, wicked little snot. God did not have to wake you up. He did not have to breathe breath into you just now. He has blessed you with life and all you can think about is yourself! You made your bed, now lay in the consequences."

"You are right — my bed. Do you think I want to have to tell my child that his big brother tried to kill us? Or that his father will not come around because it is forbidden? Better yet, how will I explain the media frenzy that will encircle the matter, not giving the child a life to live as he or she sees fit. Do not sit here and talk to me about being selfish. I wouldn't put my enemy through such drama."

Michelle sits by Natasha's knees on her right side and places her left hand in hers. Everyone is standing at the entrance, watching and hoping that Michelle will be able to reason with her. She looks into Natasha's eyes and says, "Nat, you just lost your father this year. Jeffery was shot by your gun. The doctors do not know for certain if he will be the same or if he will even remember his life. I know you were trying to defend yourself from whoever attacked you...."

"Bruce's son attacked me," Natasha interrupts and starts to cry again. She thinks about Jeffery and their date. How they had so much fun and how much she loves him. She can't believe what she has been told. She wouldn't ever think of hurting him, but she has.

Michelle continues, "You were trying to defend yourself from Bruce's son. He has not been found, and since you have been here there have been two guards on watch every day, all day. They will continue to guard you until he is captured. You are pregnant. This child is a blessing. All of the loss you have seen.... Don't you think it a good thing to have life?"

Natasha says nothing. She only turns her head to the window, closing her eyes extremely tightly as if to drown out her life. After a few moments Natasha can hear the clacking of a pair of size six-and-a-half stilettos coming closer. She hears the left side bedrail click and rustle as it is lowered, and the presence of Janet's five-foot-two frame is pressed against Natasha's good side. Janet lies facing her and places her left arm across her chest, grasping her right shoulder with her hand. When Janet lays her head on Natasha's pillow, they are face-to-face, nose-to-nose, but Natasha keeps her eyes closed. Janet lies for several minutes next to Natasha in silence as the family remains standing at the entrance, uneasy. Then Janet speaks, "Welcome back."

Natasha remains in silence with all the information she has just received weighing on her shoulders with such a burden she begins praying within herself, "Back to what? This chaos is too much for the average person. I know my actions have caused all this disarray. Lord, I still plan to live this life for You, but You are going to have to provide me with some major assistance. I cannot do this alone. I need Your help to overcome my past and to accept the repercussions of all my choices. Forgive me, God, of everything — the adultery, the usury, the malice, and for always being angry and unforgiving. God, forgive me."

Then after her thoughts cease, the calm stirring she has grown to appreciate blankets her with such peace. Then the Lord speaks, saying, "Daughter, I remember nothing of your past. You accept My Son Jesus who is the key to get to Me. Everything before you gave your life is forgiven and forgotten. I see everything that burdens your heart. The heart is where I look first. I will always be here to carry you, as long as you do not leave Me."

"Is it my breath? What's that goofy grin on your face?" Janet interrupts.

"Private thoughts, mama, private thoughts. It is going to be a long ride to recovery."

"I know you're going to be wheeled around for another week…"

"I'm not worried about that." She interrupts, "God is going to carry me through everything."

"Amen," Janet agrees.

CHAPTER TWENTY-TWO

The nurse enters Natasha's room at 7:40 sharp the following morning. "Whoa, who is awake this early?" Natasha asks, pissed at being awakened like a teenager who isn't in the mood for school.

"The nurse who has been washing your boney butt, that's who," answers Nurse Beverly, who is a busty, middle-aged woman who keeps her hair in a tight bun and wears hot pink scrubs. Looking at her makes Natasha crave cotton candy, or maybe a blow pop. "I have been dying to see you awake so I can talk to you and this not be a one-sided conversation. It has been quiet in this room for the past month, but I have kept you up-to-date the best I could. Ms. Billingsworth, it is time for your ultrasound. Let's hope this child is more of a morning person than you are."

"Let's not. I do not remember you talking to me other than yesterday when no one realized I was awake."

Nurse Beverly has the look of a grandmother or just a homely person all around, very trusting. Her hair is white at the widow's peak and her temples. It looks as if she had started highlights and then changed her mind. Natasha can't help but wonder if she suffers any back trouble from carrying around the two toddler-sized breasts on her chest. Natasha breaks away from dissecting her body type to ask, "Do you mind if I call you Bev?"

"No, everyone else does. I have never tended to a celebrity before. This is kind of exciting. You should do a tell-all book."

"I do not plan on telling anything. I am not a celebrity, just a woman whose dad was worth a fortune, and who has slept with men whose bank accounts are somewhat comparable."

Bev begins to raise the back of Natasha's bed to better prepare her for the wheelchair. The sun shines into the room and reflects off the presents that are in mounds around the room.

Natasha is amazed as she looks at the bouquets aligned against the walls around the room and the balloons in the three corners of the room. Natasha raises her right hand and places it on her heart with her mouth open in amazement.

"You have received gifts the whole time you've been in here, but your mother had to clear a ton of them out. We have regulations to keep, you know. We have the cards in the bedside table so you can read them at your leisure. Your mother brought some letters from home with a red ribbon around them. Those are also in the drawer."

Natasha can feel the blood rush to her face with the thought of Jeffery's smile. For a moment she forgets that he is lying in the same hospital, wounded and feeble. She spins around, kicking her feet over the bed's edge and leans over, stretching out her right hand as she reaches for the drawer. She pulls back quickly as the pain from her ribs sends a ripping sensation through her abdomen. Natasha screams in reaction to the pain gripping her side and closes her eyes as tightly as she can. She takes shallow breaths until the nausea subsides within her throat. After a few moments, when the pain ceases, she opens her eyes to find Bev shaking her head with her hands up as if to stop her in her actions. She also sees the guards standing in the doorway with the appearance of Agent Smith from the Matrix, with their black Armani suits and black glasses and their earpieces and guns, standing at about six foot three inches tall. Natasha has to say she is impressed.

"I am okay, Bev, you can put your hands down. Say, which guard have you chosen for yourself?"

"They look exactly alike, so it really doesn't matter. As long as they don't mind sharing me with Mr. Beverly, we are good to go."

Natasha stands for the first time in what feels like a lifetime. She insists on taking a shower before she leaves her room. Bev lets her do so with the door open in order to reach in quickly in case she needs any help. At first, Natasha objects to the idea, but then Bev reminds her, saying, "Who do you think has been giving you sponge baths and changing your waste bags, missy?" Natasha loves Bev's sense of humor. She reminds her of the older women she has always seen in the movies, like Della Reese in the movie

Harlem Nights, but without the foul language. When Natasha steps out of the shower, Bev hands her a custom-made gown compliments of Landry and the cutest pair of lime green no-slip socks she has ever seen.

"Do you want to walk? It is a good distance, but I figure if you can stand and take a fifteen-minute shower, singing every verse to every song in the movie Purple Rain, you can conquer the world."

"Bring the chair, just in case."

The guards follow Natasha as she and Bev enter the hallway. Every room door on the floor is open and the patients are as alert as they can be. Natasha remembers her father's brief stay in the hospital. She doesn't remember seeing other patients because at the time, she was wrapped up in what mattered to her the most. As she passes each room, she says a silent prayer for each patient, short and sweet, saying, "Help them, oh Lord, please help."

When they reach the elevator at the end of the hallway Bev presses seven and leans on the handles of the chair, looking at Natasha as she says, "I didn't think you to be the praying type, no offense."

"None taken. I wasn't until I accepted Jesus. My attacker helped me with the sinner's prayer. I meant every word, but he just wanted to put a bullet in my head."

"Good thing you said it from your heart, because you could be burning in hell right now."

"I am a work in progress with a ton of gray areas between that day and now."

Natasha's memory begins to fade back to the moments before the dreaded events of the attack and she thinks about Jeffery. They had had such a great time and he was just an innocent bystander. How did he get to her apartment? She finally fell in love with someone, then in the same day she put a bullet in him.

Bev looks over at Natasha and can tell by the faraway stare and the fact that she doesn't notice the elevators chime or the doors opening unto them, that she is thinking of Jeffery.

"He is on the fourth floor."

"Do we have time to stop?"

"We will make a detour after the ultrasound," Bev says, as they enter the elevator with the guards entering behind them and turning around, looking like a concealed barrier to the point that no one can see into the elevator.

"If I never visit China, I could assume this is what the Great Wall feels like," says Bev jokingly.

"I do not think the cavalry is necessary, and it is without my consent. I couldn't give an opinion at the time, but there seems to be a lot going on."

"There were reporters sneaking in to take pictures and to get interviews with the family. I do not think anyone knows you're pregnant. They know you shot Jeffery and that the suspect got away; however, they can't figure out who it is."

The elevator doors open and the guards step out into the hallway looking in opposite directions before signing to Bev and Natasha that they can step out. "To the right, Smiths," instructs Bev. As they proceed down the way, they pass by the nursery. Fifteen babies bundled in blankets lie sleeping, crying, kicking, and waving. Some are wearing blue and others are wearing pink with striped caps and wristbands. All are from different ethnicities and backgrounds. Natasha stands in amazement as she looks at how small they are and marvels that so great a sound could be made from something so little. She runs her hand down her abdomen and she can tell that where there were once abs, there is now a little bump. In shock, Natasha says, "I am going to be someone's mother. I never would have guessed that this was in my cards. I am going to suck!"

Bev chuckles and says, "Honey, the first child is known as the test run. If it survives, you are a good parent…. I'm just teasing. Every first-timer thinks that they are going to be a horrible parent, but they find later that is not true. All a child needs is love and with that love you will be everything for that child. Come on, Hollywood, we are already late."

The foursome makes another right past the nursery. As they approach Doctor Milton's office, Natasha can hear the faint sound of someone running. She stops in her tracks and turns to see what is going on. Everyone else in the posse stops and one of the guards stands between Natasha and the approaching footsteps while the other keeps watch on the opposite side of them. The footsteps get louder as the person draws closer. Smith in front of Natasha places his hand on his semi-automatic and whispers, "Stay behind me." A screeching sound comes from the pair of Nikes Janet is wearing as she comes to an abrupt stop seeing the agents in a defensive stance. She automatically puts her hands up and screams, "I am unarmed. I do not know the number to my visa off the top of my head, and I thought we were cool after I got you guys those burritos!"

"You own a pair of sneakers?" Natasha asks in amazement.

"Yes, first time wearing them. I couldn't miss this. You will be the first out of the bunch to have a baby. It is a moment and I didn't want you by yourself. Can I put my hands down?"

"I wanted to be alone."

"Yeah, but when do I ever heed your demands? You better let me come. I almost got my ass blown off by the Men in Black here."

Natasha steps from around Smith Number One and reaches out her hand. Janet grabs her hand in excitement and the party of five proceeds to the doctor's office.

Smiths know the drill. They are hired professionals who rarely speak, except for whispering to each other. Janet keeps a one-sided conversation going with them because they make her feel uncomfortable. They are actually pretty fond of Janet. The guards think it humorous how she can be talking in English and when she gets excited about a subject, reverts to her Hispanic heritage. Every now and then she will get a laugh out of Smith Two. It always startles her to the point that she almost wets herself. Once she was telling the two how she and Nathanel were lying in bed and she slobbed on his shirt when they fell asleep.

Smith Two started to laugh and out of reaction Janet hit him on the shoulder, saying, "You got to warn someone when you are about to show human emotion. Good thing we are in the hospital, you almost gave me a heart attack." Whenever she wants to get something to eat, which is often, she agrees to get them whatever she is having. Little does everyone know, they have been eating in shifts so Natasha won't be left alone for an extended period of time. Nevertheless, here are the two Bev has nicknamed 'Smiths', on guard and always alert.

The doctor isn't in his office when the girls arrive. Natasha takes a seat in front of the desk because her legs have become tired and Janet sits in the adjacent seat. Bev remains standing by the door, taking a glance at her watch then saying, "It is only eight thirty, which makes us fifteen minutes behind. Maybe he was running late to begin with."

"Maybe he stopped to get a breakfast sandwich. I could go for one right now," Janet expresses.

"Janet, you are always hungry," Natasha points out.

"In my defense, I did not have breakfast."

"Why are you wet?"

Janet looks at Natasha like she is bugging her and says, "I was rushing because I woke up late."

Doctor Milton comes in before the little spat can ignite. "Did you ladies rest well?" he asks.

"Yes," everyone says in unison, including Bev.

"Good. Let's get to it. Natasha, today is the day of the first ultrasound you will get to witness. We — Nurse Bev and I — know the sex of the baby, but today you will get to see your little miracle yourself. If you will follow me into the next room, we will get you started."

CHAPTER TWENTY-THREE

Natasha's heart pounds against her rib cage as she lies on the paper-covered table that reminds her of a cheap, extra large bucket seat with her silk gown open at the belly. Doctor Milton rubs a gel on her abdomen then looks her in the eye and asks, "Are you ready, kid?"

Natasha shakes her head to say no then closes her eyes extremely tightly. The doctor is at her right side, between Natasha and the monitor, in order to point out the child's body parts. Janet squeezes her left hand, scooting her chair closer to her bedside. Janet commands, "Look at me."

Natasha opens her eyes and faces a smiling Janet. Then she proceeds, saying, "This is your baby. You are gonna have to face it. Today might as well be the day."

Natasha swallows hard and looks at the doctor. "Ready," she announces.

"Okay, we are going to start the show." Doctor Milton presses the transducer to Natasha's lower abdomen then suddenly the room is filled with a pulsing sound.

"What is that?" Natasha asks.

"That is the baby's heartbeat. If you look here, this is the baby's head. Follow my finger. Here is the baby's arm. You can see the baby sucking the thumb. It appears the baby's toes are here." The doctor runs his finger along the screen and points at the baby's tiny feet.

"I see the baby has both legs," Natasha blurts out.

Doctor Milton runs his finger back up the screen in order to bring focus to the baby part Natasha is speaking of. "These are the legs, yes," Doctor Milton confirms.

"So what is that?" inquires Natasha.

Doctor Milton looks at Natasha with a big grin on his face and says, "Congratulations, Natasha. It is a boy."

"What?!"

Janet is crying with excitement as she explains, "Your baby has an 'outy,' and I am not talking about his belly button."

Natasha stares at the screen for several moments, not knowing how to react or what to think. A million thoughts run through her mind. She doesn't know which one to process first, nor does her mind have the time. All she can do is stare at the screen that captions another change in her entire existence.

Starting from the top she recaps. I quit my job and stopped sleeping with the boss. Found out about my father's other family. I had to bury my father. I went on a real date, and to Bible study, for God's sake. I fell in love for the first time in my life. I answered the call to salvation via Bruce's son who broke my ribs and tried to kill me. I shot the love of my life, which I found out a month later after waking from a coma. And the cake's icing today: I am five months pregnant and having a boy. Whose father is the husband of someone else, and whose son, my child's brother, tried to kill me. I think that sums it up.

Interrupting her thoughts, Janet says, "I have the printout for the ultrasound. You look tired; let's go back to your room."

"Too much for me to handle right now, I do not know where to start." Natasha looks down at her abdomen as she closes her gown, gets up from the bed, and says, "Our life is a mess, kiddo. Hope you don't hate me for it."

Taking a second look down, Natasha noticed her breasts have become quite ample. She had thought it only an illusion when she had stood in the shower, but realizes the difference is the actual truth at this very moment. All Natasha wants is to get into her own bed previous to Peagles, and wake with a clean slate. When they reach the hallway Bev grabs the wheelchair. "You must have read my mind," Natasha states. She is in the chair with Bev pushing and Janet holding her hand. Smith One leads the way while Smith Two covers the tail, and Doctor Milton runs down his schedule with Bev so she can reiterate the details later with Natasha after she takes everything in.

The doors chime on the elevator when they reach the fifth floor. As they open, Bev asks, "Are you sure you want to see Jeffery? He is non-responsive, so all you can do is look at him."

Inhaling deeply, Natasha decides, "Why not?"

"You better jump on here if you're going to ride," Bev informs the guards.

The Smiths step back into the elevator then Bev says, "Four, please."

The elevator is silent enough to hear the respirators ten floors up. Janet stands to Natasha's left and taps her foot. This reflex is a nervous habit she has had for as long as Natasha has known her. It is one of few things that annoy her about Janet.

Natasha's thoughts are going a mile a minute. It seems like an eternity passes before they reach the fourth floor. She doesn't know what to think. All she knows is that she shot him and he is critical. She assumes he is wounded in the head — at least, that is what she could gather from Doctor Milton as he gave her the rundown of her life for the past month. Will he remember me? How will he care for himself, or how could I care for him, being with child? I am having a baby! Is he going to love me after this? Does he have children?

Natasha's thoughts are racing so much that she doesn't notice they have exited the elevator and are now standing at the door of Jeffery's room. Janet interrupts her thoughts by asking, "Is it too soon, Nat?"

Natasha returns from her thoughts and realizes where she is. The guards stand on each side of the door, both facing her. Bev clears her throat due to the mounting heaviness of the situation. Moments pass before Natasha states her decision, saying, "I will go in alone." She rises from her chair with all the courage she has, reaches out her hand and places it on the handle of the door. As soon as the action is taken for her to proceed, a nurse comes up to inform them, "There is only one visitor at a time and the visit is timed. You have to wait until the other person inside leaves. They only have but a few more minutes." The nurse sees that Natasha sits in her chair again, so she doesn't think she will try to override her authority. She smiles and nods and goes on her way.

Another eternity passes, which in reality lasts only two minutes, before rustling is heard from inside the room. The door is flung open and out comes a fair-skinned, middle-aged woman with short, auburn hair. Startled at the sight of the small mob standing outside her son's room, she jumps and gasps for air, holding her chest.

"Darnit, Natasha, you are going to give me a heart attack!"

"I'm afraid I have no idea who you are. How do you know my name?"

"I am Jeffery's mother, Bernadean Pattman. I just wish we could have met under different circumstances." She reaches out her hand to shake Natasha's, but Natasha holds her head down in reaction to finding out the older woman's identity and begins to weep, apologizing for her actions and everything that transpired.

"Why do you cry like he is dead? My son will live a full life, no question. So fix your pretty face and go see him. I will be here when you return. There is a fresh gown and mask behind the door. Put it on before you get too close to him."

Bev grabs Natasha's left hand with her left and uses her right hand to support her by the elbow as if she is elderly until she gets to her feet. Bernadean has a sweet spirit, which Natasha notices right off-hand. She can't understand how she can put on the purest smile for someone who had almost taken the life of her only child.

Natasha gazes back at her in disbelief and thinks to herself, If the shoe was on the other foot, I would have my hands around the neck of the person who injured my loved one. Nevertheless, Natasha returns the smile, feeling a little lighter in spite of the mounting guilt. One thing Bernadean said rings continuously in Natasha's ears as if it was an iPod on repeat.

She enters the room with the constant beeps of machinery and the curtains half-drawn, giving the room only mild lighting to go along with the two fluorescent lights hanging over the entry way and right over Jeffery's bed. The room looks dim in comparison to the suite Natasha is residing in. The grimness of the room brings on a depressing feeling that weighs on Natasha's shoulders as if she was trying to carry four gallon jugs of water on each of her shoulders. She stands at the entry for a few moments, suited up as if she is prepped for surgery. Her feet feel as if she has on cement shoes but she knows she won't be able to rest until she sees him. She has to assess the damage, has to touch him, has to smell him, and has to be near him. He won't be able to tell her the reasons for his return to her apartment or even respond to her telling him how she feels about him, but this is something she has to do.

It takes all of her being to take the first step toward his bedside. From the door, she can only see from his waist down, as her view is blocked by a closet of fresh garments for those who visit. As Natasha takes her second step, she wonders why hers had been hanging on the back of the door. There is a wall-mounted sink with a sign taped above it that reads, "Wash hands before getting close to patient. Then put on mittens." There is a box of mittens that reminds Natasha of a box of Kleenex. Natasha looks at him somewhat side-eyed at this point. She can see Jeffery's chest as it rises and falls with the help of life support. Her heart begins to race and her knees get weak from the distress of her mind screaming at her, saying, "How could you do this to him? Your father hated the fact you owned a gun! Why didn't you get rid of it like he told you to? Now, he is dead and Jeffery will be, too, and it is on account of you."

Natasha can see Jeffery's neck. There are bandages around it so that no skin is shown. She knows she cannot do it with her eyes wide open, so she closes her eyes tightly and holds out her hand at waist level, sliding her feet slowly so as not to bump the bed too hard when she reaches her destination. Thud is the sound her fingers make when contact is made with the guardrail of the bed. Natasha takes the deepest breath she can and holds it for a few moments before releasing it out of her mouth.

Natasha had not known that this action would fog up the plastic eye guard portion of her mask, so she is startled when she opens her eyes. She lets out a small shriek and grabs onto the railing of Jeffery's bed. Looking in the direction of Jeffery's face as the smoke from her breath slowly fades away, that beautiful face that she had grown to love in such a short period of time is in plain view and more angelic than she had remembers.

She doesn't see the tubing in his mouth, the bandages wrapped all around his head, or the sensory detectors attached to his crown. None of it is apparent, because all she can see is the man that captured her heart. Her hope strengthens every time she sees his eyelids flutter. Afraid to touch him, Natasha keeps her hands on the railing and leans in closer. The doctor had said he suffered some damage to his brain and may have some memory loss, so she figures, feeling a little optimistic, that she can chat with him like Nurse Beverly had done with her to bring him up to speed.

"Jeff, there is no easy way to tell you that I shot you. So there you have it: I shot you. It was a complete accident. I was aiming for my attacker and somehow got you. This is strange to me, because I left you on the first floor of my building. We said good night and I remember getting one last glimpse of your beautiful smile as the elevator doors closed between us. It does not make sense how I shot you. I do not remember if I locked my own door but the only persons that were in my apartment were my attacker and myself. Why were you there?

"Well, in other news, my first date was with you. We went to Bible study and bowling. I had a ball and it seem to me that you enjoyed my company, too. You are such a gentleman and I can tell that given the opportunity I could trust you with my heart. You just got to get better so I can give it to you."

As soon as Natasha finishes her sentence there is a knock on her door. The noise startles Natasha into a flashback and she turns around, putting her hands before her face to protect herself. An unfamiliar voice rings out, "Your time is up." Natasha releases the breath she did not realize she was holding with such intensity that it seems she is drowning. She is overcome by such fear that she faints. The slow motion of this dramatic scene would be perfect if it was an old movie, but this is not a movie. This is Natasha's reality.

"What was that noise?" Bernadean inquires of the nurse.

"Wait here," the nurse demands and enters the room alone. Moments later, a doctor and another nurse are rushing toward the small mob that lingers outside of Jeffery's hospital room. Every eye that dwells in the heads of Natasha's posse, including Bernadean, widens two centimeters with panic written on every face.

"Could someone please tell us what the hell is going on?" Janet demands.

The nurse who was running with the doctor stops to calm the restless loiterers who look as if they are on the brink of breaking the door down. She stands among the group on the threshold of the door with her hands up and says in a monotone, "Natasha has fainted. It seems everything is okay. The doctor is going to have a look at her, then Nurse Bev will take her back to her room where she can rest. Jeffery has not been disturbed. In fact, the nurse said it doesn't look like she attacked him again. That's great news."

Bernadean's chest expands broadly as anger raises her blood pressure, made evident by the flaring of her nostrils and the increased redness in her cheeks. She says, "Listen here, you ignorant little wench. If I so much as overhear you cracking those lame wisecrack jokes concerning my son Jeffery or Natasha, I will have your job. Make yourself useful and see what's taking so damn long if the only thing she did was faint."

The nurse's already tiny five-foot-three posture has effectively been diminished by three more inches as she scurries into the room as Bernadean had instructed. "I hate when these whores make me have to act ugly in public. Saying some foolishness like that. Have onlookers questioning if I really love the Lord."

Bev just nods her head and adds, "She has only been here four days. That might have been the only thing she could think to say. You have to raise a little hell to get some peace sometimes."

CHAPTER TWENTY-FOUR

Bernadean Pattman had been your typical single mother raising her son alone after Jeffery's father passed away when he was three. Mr. Pattman had attached himself to her five-eight Coke bottle frame in high school; the year was nineteen sixty-eight. Every picture from their teens until his death showed the two photographed together. Inseparable and in love had been the two.

There was nothing their parents could say or do to keep them apart; whether grounded or forbidden they still wound up entangled in one another. No one was surprised when the day after graduation the two went to the municipal court and tied the knot. Jeffery didn't come along until the two were thirty-three. She tried her best to tell her son all she could about his father so he could get a sense of who he had been and how much he had meant to Bernadean. Jeffery knows about every moment that was special, sorrowful, and secretive in the marriage of his father and mother. The village of family from both sides, including church members, played a major role in Jeffery's upbringing. He was well-educated, well-cultured, and well-loved.

***

The house is filled with smoke as Natasha tries crawling from her bedroom to the exit of her apartment. Her chest feels as if it is on fire and she cannot see in front of her due to the smoke. She is only a few feet away from the exit when her lungs become completely empty of clean air and she collapses on the floor, dead.

The screams coming from the once unconscious Natasha blare in the ears of Janet and everyone on the same floor of the hospital. The Smiths are in the room and on guard with guns drawn and checking the body count in the room. Doctor Milton comes in a few moments later at high speed to find himself with two 9mm guns aimed directly at his head. He stops in his tracks and immediately raises his hands. "Doctor Milton on duty," he says sarcastically. Smith One and Smith Two put away their weapons and chuckle at the doctor's statement.

Doctor Milton administers the same physical he did when Natasha woke from her coma. Agitated, she knocks his hands out of her face. She begins to state with plenty of bass in her voice, "I was having a bad dream. I am not blind. All my vitals are normal. Get that light away from me!"

"I guess we should start paying you and throw in a white coat," replies Doctor Milton, mildly amused. Janet climbs onto the foot of Natasha's bed and patiently waits until everyone leaves the room. When the door closes behind Smith Two, Janet looks Natasha in the eye and asks, "Was it too much seeing Jeffery today? I mean, you just woke up yesterday and then today you see your baby for the first time. You see Jeffery and then faint. Honey, move slowly. You have to think about the baby."

"I had a dream my apartment was on fire. I was trying to crawl out but fell dead before I hit the door."

Janet sighed and said in her Spanish accent, "Drama in your reality and in your dreams. Tash, you must take it easy. I wonder why your place was on fire. When you think of it, dreams are like messages from God that need to be decoded, mysteries from the biggest Master ever. He might have been trying to tell you something."

"Janet, I have no clue what I am doing. I do not know how to be what God wants. I do not know how to be a mother. I don't know how to be anyone's girlfriend, and the way my rap sheet is looking, I wouldn't date me either. Not that being in a relationship is top of my list, but I was willing, for the first time, to open up."

Even as Natasha finishes her last sentence, her mind races at high speed thinking, *It has been a month and some days and I never considered moving. To think about it, it might be a crime scene. Shit, Junior is still on the loose and may still be in the mood for revenge. God, can I say 'shit?' Should I move? What would I do about my new furniture if I move? Hell, I* just redecorated! Can I say 'hell?' Help! My God, I feel like I am drowning in my thoughts.

"Natasha Billingsworth! Are you in there?" shouts Janet, trying to get Natasha back in the room. "Whatever you decide, we are here for you. You are stressing about things that you need not worry about, *chica*. I got a call from Felicia! She will be in this afternoon to see you. The people around you are the people who love you. Anything that doesn't need you there physically, we can take care of it."

Felicia. Sad to say, but Natasha hadn't thought about the one missing piece from her circle of friends. She can't remember if she last saw her the night of the party at Peagles or at the funeral. Felicia has always been the friend with whom you had the occasional lunch, the occasional phone call, and the occasional outing. No matter how little she and Felicia communicate, she finds comfort in knowing if she needs anything she can call her and she or her husband will handle the things she needs, no questions asked.

"It will be good to see Felicia. I was always surprised she would bring her husband around me and even not mind us being alone together," says Natasha, wearing a face that expresses her wonder.

"I always said she was *mucha loca* for doing that, but she said she believed you had enough love and respect for her that you wouldn't do that," states Janet matter-of-factly. Then she continues, "She also said you know she frequents the gun range and wouldn't mind exercising her right to bear arms on anyone who tried."

They both burst into laughter so loudly they don't hear Felicia enter the room. She stands there for a moment before the two look in her direction. Clearing her throat, Felicia announces, "I have arrived, and you heifers better not have said a word about me in my absence that you cannot repeat in my presence."

Smith Two is standing at the door to make sure Natasha actually knows the beauty. "It's okay, *gato*, we know her. Hey, in a few I'm going to the sandwich place, did you want anything? Better yet, I am in the mood for pizza."

"Pizza sounds great. One of us could grab it, but it's on you this time only because you keep calling me a cat," states Smith Two.

"It is the way you move, man. Calculated, like you have walked these halls all your life and you know them like the back of your hand, strange."

"You two want to take this outside? I need to catch my good buddy up on what we were saying about her and all the happenings for the past day. Pizza does sound excellent. Get me one with everything on it. I am starving!"

Felicia looks surprised, then states, "For years, you have only eaten pineapples on your pizza, but today you choose to have every topping possible?" She and Janet then lock eyes. Janet rises from her seat to exit to get the day's delicacies. She extends her arm with her hand palm-up, then says as she smacks her free hand on top, "Put it there!" Felicia gives her fifty dollars and rolls her eyes. Janet is closing the door behind her but it isn't fully shut, so those inside hear Janet say, "Lunch is on Felicia today, everybody!"

"There is no sign of a baby bump for you to be five months. I was sure this was a crazy crank on Janet's part. Are you really pregnant?"

"All jokes aside, I am knocked up."

"The father, please tell me it is cutie from the party? Wait, that would be impossible since you just met him," Felicia claims.

"In a perfect world, yeah, but in this reality it is my old boss's child."

"Damn! Forgive me, God. Does he know? Wait… you just woke up… no one really knows anything, huh?"

"Nope. What I do know is who tried to kill me, and it is my unborn child's half-brother. It is crazy the mess I have made of my life. Do you believe as he was allowing me to have my last words while in the land of the living, he led me to the Lord? We said the prayer. I meant it. I know that I know I meant it."

"Well, praise God you would have at least made it in the gates if that was your appointed time."

"You never think about your end, or should I say the end until it is right in front of you. I was careless of others and destructive to myself. Now, I am back from limbo, pregnant and with the news that I pulled the trigger on my new love, Jeffery."

"How is he?"

"He is in this same hospital, still critical. I went to see him today…"

"You went to see him?" asks Felicia, cutting Natasha off in mid-sentence.

"Yes, I did. I had to see it for myself. After the ultrasound, we…"

"Ultrasound?"

"Stop cutting me off! Yes, after the ultrasound we detoured to his room in ICU."

"Let me get this straight. Today you have not been awake longer than twenty-four hours and you have seen your unborn child for the first time, seen Jeffery in ICU, and you are sitting here in this bed like you are on vacation. I would be in a padded wagon on my way to the looney bin."

"It is a boy. Also, I met Jeffery's mother today."

"I feel like I am in the Twilight Zone. Last I heard, you were meeting your brothers from another mother in the Hamptons. You found out that your ex-boss's assistant was the fiancée of the guy you slept with in all that wedding drama. Your father passing, God rest his soul. I can't keep up, honey."

"Felicia, you are just an onlooker. I am living this every second of this day and any others God decides to let follow hereafter. If someone had shown me this portion of my life, I would have called them a liar."

"How are you doing with baby?"

"I am still feeling a discomfort with the ribs still in the healing process." Natasha begins to look off into the distance past those four walls and continues, saying, "I heard the heartbeat. That rapid thumping that if it were bass from the neighbor's surround sound I would be pulling my hair out. There is a living, breathing boy in me. His conception was truly a mistake, and shameful. Honestly, I still have thoughts of putting him up for adoption. I do not want to have to have the conversation about his father, what happened to his brother, and his mother believing just like Aunt FeFe in her right to bear arms."

"'Aunt Felicia?' Nat, I would have never have expected those words or even the thought of children to come out of your mouth. You talking of God and actually thinking of someone but yourself is such a change, but more so an assurance that God still answers prayers. He doesn't move as soon as you pray in some cases, but He moves when necessary."

"I think of Jeffery. Since I woke up the second time, all I see when I blink is him lying in ICU fighting for his life."

"What do you mean, since you woke up the second time?" Felicia inquired.

"I fainted when I saw him."

"He was that bad?"

"No, I believe it was post-traumatic stress. I heard a noise and had a vivid flashback. Fe, what am I doing? Really, what am I doing? I practically ruined him, the child, and Bruce's family. All my life all I have done was made a mess of things. It is through God alone that you all are still my friends and have tolerated my nonsense all these years."

Felicia, also known as Fe to her closest friends, looks upon her distressed friend and, filled with compassion, says, "Nat, to be honest with you, there were many days I wanted to throw you away. There is definitely a God, because without Him I would never befriend someone like you. I would prepare my heart, mind, and soul to put you in my past, but I just couldn't. Jesus saved our friendship. He gave me patience, love, compassion, and longsuffering. People say that's what you get when you marry. I can testify that you can get these things from someone you rarely see. It's not like we hung out enough to make a difference, but the little time we talked and came together made a big change in me. Those changes, Natasha, brought out the best in me."

Natasha shifts her weight from her back to her hip as she leans more on her right side. She suddenly feels uncomfortable. The discomfort had felt minor as Felicia spoke, but is now inching its way closer and closer to the front of Natasha's mind. There is this mounting sense to call for help. Natasha shakes her head at the thought because she can't pinpoint this sense of nausea and the need to take off running. The urge grows in her to the point that she feels her stomach disagree with its normal function.

"Are you okay, Nat?" Felicia asks out of concern for the fact that her friend's face is suddenly turning green.

"I don't know."

Natasha feels as if someone is grabbing her attention. She suddenly looks toward the exit, only to find she is no longer in her room at Lenox Hill Hospital. This place is foreign, ancient in architecture. There is music playing with an Italian rhythm and the beat of the city is vibrant as the people who are passing don't notice Natasha's presence at all. As Natasha makes a full one hundred-eighty degree-turn, she finally figures out where she is — Milan.

The city is beautiful in its entire splendor, but Natasha can't help but wonder why she is here. The answer is revealed when the revolving stops right in front of an enormous sign with lights flashing, revealing the building where Fall Fashion Week will be held. Suddenly, Natasha feels a jerk to her right and she is plunged into darkness. She can't see an inch in front of or behind her. She is about to yell out, but the sound of whimpering catches her attention.

Natasha is afraid to move, fearing she might fall over or cause a disturbance. There is another cry and Natasha strains to listen again. Footsteps are echoing overhead as if she is in the basement. The whimpering falls silent as the steps grow closer. Threatening, malicious, and vindictive are the steps that become a blaring alarm as they come down some stairs. Natasha counts to twelve until the footsteps come to a halt. Then, frightening enough, the darkness becomes light. In reaction, Natasha places her hand over her eyes to block the sudden flash; the scream faded into the distance.

Natasha realizes she is no longer in the place but back in her hospital room, hand still over her eyes and Felicia still looking at her as if she has lost her mind.

"Welcome back, Nat. I would have called the doctor if you'd stopped blinking. What is going on with you?" Felicia inquires.

"I think I was just in Milan at Fashion Week and someone, a woman, was in a dark room crying. I think she was being held against her will, hence the whimpering and scream when the door opened."

Felicia moves from her chair and takes a seat at the foot of Natasha's bed. She looks upon her friend as if she has had a moment of enlightenment. Natasha feels like a sideshow freak as her dear friend looks upon her. Then after moments of silence, Felicia gives her some insight, stating, "You are a seer. There are people in the Bible that dream dreams and see visions. These vessels of God are called seers."

"Felicia, this is a bit deep for a subject I know nothing of. I wouldn't know what a seer would look like if one walked up to me, slapped me, and then asked me if I saw it."

The two can't help but chuckle after Natasha's joke, but Felicia knows her friend, and she knows how to maneuver past her humor. "Seriously, Nat, some people are saved the majority of their life and God will show them nothing, whether asleep or awake; but you, my dear friend, have a gift. It could have been there the whole time," Felicia educates her friend.

"So what if I am this seer person? What do I do with the information? I dreamed of being trapped in a burning room, now it's a girl in Milan crying and captured against her will."

"You have to ask God to teach you up how to use your gift, and how to interpret what you see," Felicia informs her.

Natasha exhales really deeply then says, "This is too much for a lifetime, let alone a few days. I am getting more and more tired with every piece of information I receive. I am starting to regret waking up. God has got to teach me to be saved, a mother, and a seer. I think He has His work cut out for Him with being saved alone. What am I doing?"

As soon as the cloud of being overwhelmed begins to creep in Natasha's direction, Bev comes into the room quietly, walking softly as if Natasha is sleeping. She suggests that Felicia leave so Natasha can get some much-needed rest. They had had an early morning and even though Natasha has been quick in her thoughts, she has only been out of a coma for a little over thirty hours. The two friends embrace and Felicia leaves her girlfriend and thanks Bev for doing a spectacular job tending to her friend. The two women shake hands. Felicia smiles back at her friend as she exits. Bev announces, "It's been a long time since I got a Holy Ghost handshake."

"What's a Holy Ghost handshake?"

Bev flashes a big smile, delighted as if teaching something to a child, then says, "It is when someone shakes your hand and leaves money in it. These shakes come all of a sudden but are much appreciated. Thank You, Jesus!"

CHAPTER TWENTY-FIVE

Bev spends a few moments giving Natasha her prenatal vitamins. She fluffs her pillows, making sure she is comfortable. It is high noon, so Bev walks over to the large window and begins to draw the shade when Natasha asks, "Should I wait now or later to tell the police I know who attacked me?"

"We alerted the police as soon as you were awake. You would think New York's finest would have been here to question you about the night of the attack by now. Gunshot wounds have to be reported immediately," replies Bev. As soon as she completes her sentence, the phone in the room rings. Natasha turns to her right to reach the phone on the bedside stand but winces when she realizes her ribs are still tender.

"Child, hold still, it is only the first ring and it is not like you are going anywhere fast. Let me get it." Bev walks from the window to Natasha's side, all the while saying, "We were told not to disclose any information about you since you got here so the only people that know you are here are your family. I would have told you sooner but the room was so quiet for the month it must have slipped my mind."

Bev takes a deep breath then answers the phone, saying, "Nurse Beverly speaking." Moments pass, then Bev retorts to whoever is on the line, "You could have paged me in the hallway so it wouldn't disturb Ms. Billingsworth. Ringing the phone was a crazy alternative. I will be there in a moment. Thank you." She hangs up and huffs, "New hires." Natasha gives a chuckle that is cut short because the phone rings a second time. She then starts to laugh because she can see Bev's irritation mount due to the back-to-back calls. "You need your rest. This better not be this idiot, sorry, woman again," states Bev with a fierceness even Natasha is a little nervous about.

She says a second time as if she is in a scene of a movie and she was being asked to do this line for the thousandth time, "Nurse Beverly speaking." There is a brief pause before Bev says sharply, "I will allow only a few minutes, because your sister needs her rest."

She hands the phone to Natasha, who answers, "Hello."

"Natasha, it is great to see you are still among the living."

A chill goes up Natasha's spine due to her recognition of the caller's voice. Her thought process doesn't allow her to rehearse what she would like to say to the father of her unborn child. She hasn't thought about a name, birthdays, visitation, or anything involving Bruce. Here he is on the other end of her receiver managing to sound genuinely concerned, but why?

"Bruce?" asks Natasha, pretending she does not know exactly who is on the other end. She knows how to suck the information out of him and depending on his answer she knows his location and whether she has to decipher code words.

"Yes, Natasha, this is Bruce. Did you hear what I said? I am glad you are okay. Please forgive the way everything went down on the day of your resignation. But more importantly, forgive my son."

He has said her name, which indicates he is at work in his office using a private line that only she and Ashley know about. Natasha thinks for a moment about how to word her questions to get the answers she really wants out of Bruce. His tone is soft as if he is trying to soothe a toddler. "Hello, are you there, Natasha?"

"I'm here. Why did you ask me to forgive your son?"

Bruce takes a deep breath then sighs, saying, "I know what happened. He told me everything. He was outraged at the media putting such a scandal on things. His mother moved out and didn't take the children with her. He came to my house that night and confessed everything that happened. Junior told me he assaulted you and he was about to pull the trigger when a man came in and jumped him from behind. You fired your weapon but missed Junior and hit whoever was trying to save you. He ran from the apartment without his weapon and with both of you unconscious on the floor."

Natasha is in tears and Beverly doesn't know who she is talking to, but she knows Natasha only has two brothers and the person on the phone is upsetting her. She goes to pull the phone from Natasha but she jerks her head away.

"Listen to me, Bruce. If you think I am not going to go to the police with this, you are wrong. Your son violated me and was prepared to take my life. I am paying for what I did to your family, and I am truly sorry for breaking up your home. I had no right…"

"It was broken before you. Our situation was just the straw that broke the camel's back, I guess. Junior has always had emotional problems, even as a child. We put him in boarding and military schools but he always managed to get kicked out for one reason or another. Mourna wanted more kids after three but could barely carry any of them full term. Our love affair went on far too long and yes, we should not have started it, but what is done is done. I am terribly sorry that this has happened, but I must ask if you would please refrain from pressing charges against my son. He will not get away clean, but he will have a chance."

All of a sudden, there is a faraway sound as if someone has cleared their throat into the receiver. Natasha is livid at the realization that Bruce would have him there listening to their conversation while he pleads his cause. The heat of her anger rises from her toe nails to the top of her head. She states through clenched teeth, "I am not afraid of what you think you can do to me. You are only a man — a weak, pathetic man who did not get enough attention from your mommy and daddy. Listen to me carefully, because I am not going to repeat myself. There is nothing you can do to hurt me. You will be prosecuted and there is nothing you can do to change that. Most importantly, Junior, I forgive you, and thank you for leading me to God. Thank you for helping me escape eternal damnation. I pray you find your way."

There is a murky stillness on the phone that makes Natasha's bones tremble with adrenaline. Breaking the silence, Junior states, "I will not allow you to have peace. I will wreak havoc in your life as long as I can. I don't care who I have to touch but I will get to you. You will want to die for the pain I will cause you."

The entire time Junior is speaking, Bruce is yelling, "That's enough!" Like the disobedient child he is, he never stops. It occurs to Natasha that if he is at the office then Ashley would have seen him enter. No one outside of Bev, Felicia, and the family knows who had done this to her. Ashley would probably speak and be polite, not knowing he has been guilty all along. Entering and exiting the office like he has done nothing wrong.

Natasha grows tired of the barks and says, "Listen carefully, because this is for the both of you and the rest of your family. There will be a new addition. I am pregnant and it is a boy. Bruce, you are the father!" Natasha's disconnecting the line is an indication that this is not the end of the crazy fiasco, but only the beginning of a wild ride. Bev is standing over Natasha rubbing her head at this point. She looks as if her heart hurts from being on the outside looking in on the situation. The phone rings a third time and since Natasha is still gripping the receiver in the cradle, she answers, "Yes?" because she knows deep down Junior will not let her have the last say, word, and definitely not the last laugh.

"When you think you're protected, you won't be. The Men in Black will not be around you forever. Those two can't protect all of your family and friends twenty-four seven. I will take them down one by one. Then guess what? I'm coming for you. I am going to rip that bastard child from your womb and allow you to look at it before you take your last breath. Tsk, tsk. Your boy toy is barely hanging on as we speak. Who's going to protect him?"

The dial tone is all Natasha can comprehend. Her mind spins into a web of thoughts moving too fast for her understanding. A distant echo is all she can hear of Beverly calling to her to see if she is okay.

"I am fine. I need some rest."

CHAPTER TWENTY-SIX

The clacking of stilettos, and more specifically the tempo of the feet whose body they are carrying, is a signature sound to the ears of Felicia. Moments later, Janet almost slams into her as she rounds the corner. "I knew it was you from the all-too-familiar sound of your heels. Do you own a pair of flats?" Felicia asks jokingly.

"As a matter of fact, I do. You missed my sneakers yesterday along with the ultrasound."

"Those are two things I thought I would never hear or see in my life — Natasha pregnant and you in sneakers," Felicia states.

Janet shifts her weight to her left leg and folds her arms over her chest. This is her signature "I have dirt on you pose," which is a look she only sees her give Natasha when she is dead wrong. The only thing Felicia can wonder is if she knows. After giving Felicia the once-over, she asks, "Did you tell Natasha?"

Felicia's heart begins to race and her palms become sweaty from her nervousness. She knows that if she says "No," Janet will turn her around and force her to tell Natasha what she should have told her when she had introduced her and Jeffery at the Peagles party. If she says "Yes," Janet in random conversation will mention it, thinking Natasha already knows. So she replies, "Yes. Just moments ago I told her."

"My Nat. So much going on and I had to find out you and Jeffery were an item through his mother. She said she didn't know you and Natasha were close and she was glad that you could overlook the fact that your best friend was dating, shot, and almost killed your ex-fiancé. She was in the lobby when I was coming in with the food. Why didn't you say something sooner?"

"First off, I am married and still in love with my husband. Secondly, you had to be at the Peagles party. Seeing Natasha genuinely smile at a man and enjoy his company was a first. Jeff and I never had that much fun together and the relationship only lasted two and a half years. He is a great guy. I just hope he makes it out of this alive and with his right mind. Natasha should get the man of her dreams, don't you think?"

There is a pause of agreement between the two, then Felicia's thought flashes into her mind in an instant, leading her to say, "Wait, you said you came back with food and there is none in your hands. There were no guards at the door when I left."

"What the hell are you trying to say, Felicia?" Janet's face turns dark as the anger boils in her cheeks.

"I am saying Natasha is alone. Why are both guards away from her door? Shouldn't one be there at all times?"

The two run as fast as their legs can carry them. For the first time in their acquaintance, the two have mixed feelings toward each other concerning their sincerity to Natasha. If there were a woman that deserved to get what she had coming, it was certainly Natasha, but somewhere beyond the caution tape, Janet and Felicia decided to love their friend instead.

***

The silence is not an unusual thing at the manor. Michele had grown accustomed to being alone after Natasha went off to college. Bryant was always away at the office, on business trips. Those business trips, it had been revealed, were more for the purposes of pleasure. Two sons and a mistress' worth of pleasure, although Michelle had to admit she had actually grown fond of her new family.

Sitting alone in the house for the past few days had only left Michelle with time to think. As she sits in her favorite room in the house, the memories come flooding back to her. The sunroom glows with radiance as noon approaches. The wicker furniture with floral cushions would remind anyone of the cover of a Home and Garden magazine with the décor. Her coffee cup leaves a ring on the side table as she takes a slow sip, inhaling the hazelnut and vanilla concoction.

As she reflects, Michelle cannot pinpoint a time in her life when she has ever been truly over-the-moon happy. She was glad to know Bryant had money and would give her and her brother the stability they needed and the income they never had. After the death of their parents she had taken on the sole responsibility of their survival. She didn't want child services to break them up, so she lied about her age, dropped out of high school and went to work at a gentlemen's club in a neighboring city. It was certainly far from her dreams of becoming a doctor. Michelle had wanted to travel to poverty-stricken countries and give them the healthcare they needed. She had wanted to save the world, and more importantly, she believed she could. It never crossed her mind to be an opportunist. Her family was poor, yes, but Michelle had dreams enough to get them out of the slums, and into some great living. She would keep her abasement by knowing that there was someone else out there that was surviving far worse conditions than she was.

The disappointment of Michelle's coffee cup becoming empty is interrupted by the ringing of her doorbell. She is not expecting company and with the last month of events she has hardly been home. When she looks out of the door's beveled-glass side panels, she sees Melvin Junior standing at her door looking the spitting image of her deceased brother. She can't remember the last time she has seen him. The death of his father, the death of his wife, and the opening of his restaurants have kept him an introvert. Nevertheless, here he is standing at her front door. Melvin is holding a box in his right hand and is putting the other up to ring the bell a second time when Michelle finally opens the door.

"Junior, what brings you to my neck of the woods and off work?"

"I had a free day, finally, and decided to bring up some groceries and just to see how you were holding up," Melvin claims.

"Come on in, son."

They walk through the foyer in the direction of the kitchen. Melvin looks at the interior like it is his first time in the residence. Technically, it has been about a decade since his presence was felt on this estate. They enter the kitchen and Melvin places the package on the counter. He starts to unload its contents on the large island and Michelle just stands there and watches. She can't help but wonder why he is really here. He never calls, never emails – not that Michelle knows how to check her email – nor does he ever write.

"I wanted to talk to you about something that has been on my mind for years," Melvin says while he is still pulling the last contents out of his box. "I remember things from my childhood that are not easy to cope with. My father was very grateful for you getting him out of Mississippi, but I just can't for the life of me understand the way you treated my mother after my sister was born. Landry pretty much dismissed the torment because she has always loved her cousin past anything you could ever do to her. I'd rather not come around because I have been so angry about how you accused my mother of being a slut, and said that Landry was not his child. I came today to get this off my chest so I can have some peace and move on."

Michelle takes a deep breath and realizes she had forgotten about the damage she had caused. She knew her brother wouldn't do combat with her because she was the reason his lifestyle had changed for the better. The events of Michelle's life have brought her to a certain place, a place where she needs to search out who she really is. She is rich, she is single, and she does not have a clue what she wants to do with the rest of her life. No matter how long or short it is.

"I do owe you and your sister an apology. I was mean, and cruel, and assuming. Your mother was a beautiful person, but in Mississippi, black people do not have babies like Landry. I should not have been such a bigot to my own flesh and blood. I am sorry, Melvin."

There is an awkward silence with air so thick it is hard for Michelle to breathe. She can't read Melvin like she could his father. This is mostly due in part to the fact that she doesn't really know her nephew. They never bonded and never got to know one another and it was solely her fault.

"I thought this would be different. There is a large sense of relief but... I don't know what to expect. I guess we will move on," Melvin confirms.

Melvin and Michelle talk like they are the best of friends who haven't seen each other in years. He puts on his chef cap and prepares a meal good enough to put a price tag on. They finally get to discuss his father and how they were brought up in Mississippi. By the end of their meal, Michelle finally understands what she is to do with the rest of her existence.

"I think I want to move to Argentina. As bad as Janet got on my blasted nerves with that blabbing, it is still a beautiful language to me, and I think I'll learn it before I move."

Melvin looks at Michelle with his head cocked to the side and says, "You are really serious?"

"Yep, I'm gon' do it."

CHAPTER TWENTY-SEVEN

It was been two weeks since Landry has seen her favorite cousin and although she has a busy schedule, her thoughts are all toward Natasha and all that has happened. It has been more than once that it has run across Landry's mind that Natasha is reaping what she has sown. Landry can't believe the thought and quickly pushes it out. She has another week before Milan's Fashion Week, and she is a featured designer. Her phone hasn't stopped ringing since her debut. She has had to expand her company and hire an assistant to help her keep up with herself as well as her sales. Dry Greens is set to be in a department store or boutique in all fifty states. Online sales increased sixty-five percent after she hired a marketing team.

Out of all the chaos, Landry knows she needs to see her cousin more than anything. She knows she hasn't been awake but a couple of days, and truth be told, she doesn't know how to approach her after something so dramatic. She doesn't know how to downplay her feelings in order not to hurt someone else's. Landry only acquired two percent of the sensitivity hormone of which most women have a large quantity. Nevertheless, here she is outside of the lobby of Lenox Hill Hospital, wondering if she should just leave.

Landry enters the lobby and takes a deep breath of sterilized air and walks up to the counter. She asks the nurse behind the counter, "Could I have the room number of Natasha Billingsworth, please?"

"May I see some identification?"

Landry hands the stern nurse her driver's license and waits while the nurse types her information into the computer. After a few moments, she then says, "Room five zero six."

As Landry walks the halls of the fifth floor, she starts to have memories of her father and his last days, along with those of her mother and Melvin Junior's deceased wife. The feeling of loss drapes her shoulders, bringing about a sudden sadness. She stands outside of Natasha's door for a few moments before she reaches for the handle. Before she can turn it to enter the room, Bev approaches her with a big smile on her face. "You must be Landry. Natasha described you perfectly."

"Really? Are you her nurse?"

"I am. My name is Bev. Natasha has had a festive day and she is getting some rest."

"What have I missed?"

"Well, for starters she had her ultrasound this morning. It was hard but she is strong. The family visits on a regular basis. This is the first time today the guards have been off their post. I guess Janet brought them back the food they wanted. Another friend came to visit. Beautiful girl, she looked like a model. There was a call that seems to have upset Natasha, but she said nothing else, just went to sleep."

"That is festive. I knew there were guards but if one of them is not outside the door at all times then that defeats the purpose, don't you think?"

"It has been very little commotion and nothing alarming has happened so I guess they have gotten comfortable."

Beverly finished her last sentence just in time to see the elevator doors open and Janet, along with Felicia, running in their direction. Janet looks confused and Beverly is standing like a mother hen with her hands on her hips. The two stop right in front of Natasha's door, trying to catch their breath.

Landry looks at them with her palms up and asks, "What has you two in such a hurry? Did you see the guards?"

Out of breath and with a look of frantic panic, Janet states, "I brought them food. Maybe they felt it was okay if she was with Felicia. Felicia and I realized Natasha was alone so we ran back."

Bev looks at all the girls and realizes she took a restroom break while doing her rounds. From their accounts, she can guess that Natasha has been unattended for at least ten minutes.

In reaction, she takes off into Natasha's room with the small mob following in reflex. Standing at the foot of Natasha's bed is a man in a white gown with matching socks and boxer shorts. He has traces on his hand where an IV used to be. The thing that separates him from a lost wanderer is the semiautomatic weapon he has aimed at Natasha, who is sleeping and unaware. At once the women charge the man, who appears to be in a daze. He turns in their direction to open fire. Bev reaches him first, using all her body weight to tackle the man to the floor. There is a shot fired on impact.

The sound sends a piercing ring in Natasha's ears that wakes her out of her sound sleep. Bev repeatedly punches the attacker until blood is coming from his mouth. Felicia grabs the weapon, which had been flung above the assailant's head. She touches Bev's shoulder and yells, "That's enough!" When Bev gets to her feet she is panting, trying to catch her breath, and sweating profusely. The man is still lying on the floor because Felicia, who is obviously capable of pulling the trigger, has the weapon aimed right between his eyes.

"You move and I shoot," Felicia informs him with a face as sure as Clint Eastwood.

In all the room's stirring, Landry suddenly yells out, "Janet has been shot!"

Bev goes over to her quickly to assess the wound. Blood is oozing out of Janet's lower left abdomen. Bev grabs Landry's hand and places it over the wound. "Keep your hand there and apply a little pressure. Do not move until I tell you to," demands Bev.

Natasha sits up too quickly. The intense pain from broken ribs moves from her midsection to her toes. She feels as if she is going to vomit due to the agony. She presses the nurse's button and grabs the phone, which was in the bed with her, and dials the police.

Felicia continues her stance over the gunman. Bev grabs some supplies from the drawers at the sink. Pulling on a pair of rubber gloves and grabbing gauze, she goes back to Janet. She relieves Landry of her duty and tends to Janet's wound. Moments later, a nurse comes in with Smiths One and Two in tow. Astonished at the sight that greets them, the Smiths pull out their weapons. Smith One aims at Felicia and Smith Two aims at the assailant on the floor.

Angered by the obvious intention of the guard, Felicia yells, "You dumb bastard! If I wanted to kill the person you were supposed to be protecting she would be dead by now. He is the intruder." She jabs the

handgun in the direction of the man in the white gown on the floor with his
hands up.

A little embarrassed, Smith One points his firearm in the appropriate
direction and reaches for his phone to call the police. Natasha sees that he
is trying to dial and informs him flatly, "We have already called the cops.
Your job is done. As soon as they get here, you are dismissed from your
duties. My mother will handle the payment and contracts. Thank you so
much for your time."

"Janet, the bullet only grazed you. You will need a few stitches but
nothing to worry about," assures Bev as she gets her to her feet. Bev gives
orders to the nurse, instructing her where to take Janet for treatment and
who to see at this hour. The nurse agrees and escorts Janet out, walking
past the guards to the exit.

Bev removes her gloves as she walks to Natasha's bed and asks how
she is doing. Natasha appears a little pale, like she has seen a ghost. Bev
checks her vitals and makes sure all is as normal as can be. "Try to relax,
Natasha. Your blood pressure is high and that isn't good for you right
now," suggests Bev.

"How can I relax when someone tried to kill me again! I have no idea
what my mother paid these two, but I pray she gets a refund. Peace, after all
this hell, I just want some peace. I'm not sure what that feels like in the first
place, but I was sure I was about to get some before all this shit... stuff...
happened."

Bev looks over her left shoulder in Felicia's direction. She is still
standing over the gunman. The sun starts to appear through the cracks of
the curtains, illuminating her strands, and Bev jokingly says, "You have
Colombiana over here; I think you can breathe." They both laugh and
moments later the police arrive with Detective Robert Allen leading the
officers.

Detective Allen has been one of New York's finest for a quarter of a
century. He started with the police academy at the age of twenty-one.
Seeing all of the crime in his city as a youth only made him want to protect
the innocent. Robert Allen is solid in stature, with hair that is graying at the
temples. His face is serious but his eyes are delicate, very trusting. He is the
image of every girl's favorite uncle — one that will protect, but still is able
to have a few laughs and put his feet up.

Allen takes in the scenery and says, "Okay, okay, so everyone has guns. Let's see who is registered. It looks like a standoff. Buddy on the floor, I hate to tell you this, but you are outnumbered."

Allen motions toward the gunman on the floor so the two officers following him can apprehend the stranger. They seat him in the chair in the corner of Natasha's room and cuff him to the chair. The gunman, dressed in the white gown, does not make a sound. Bev notices he has on a hospital bracelet and asks, "What is the name on the bracelet?"

"Billy Trudy," One of the officers calls out. "He is fifty-six and he is allergic to penicillin," he completes.

Detective Allen walks over to Natasha so he can formally introduce himself. Standing six one and about two hundred-ten pounds, he is fit for a detective. He looks over at Felicia and asks, "Lara Croft, could you please give the weapon to the other officer? We will have to take you downtown for prints when we are done here." He then turns his attention to the Smiths and demands, "Step outside, please."

He pulls a pad and pen from a pocket in his coat to take a few notes. Allen volunteers his hand to Natasha, which she shakes with no problem since the pain has subsided.

"I am Detective Allen, Robert Allen. It is strange that I was already headed this way because I had just gotten news this morning that you were awake. I'm glad to see you on this floor and not in the morgue. I will be handling your case until we catch your attacker. Well, Billy here made it a little easy for us."

"He is not my initial attacker," clarifies Natasha.

"Didn't he just try to kill you? It looks like it was about to be another world war in here."

"Billy is number two. He was probably paid a great deal of money to try to finish what Bruce Junior started."

"Bruce Junior? Isn't your boss named Bruce Wilson? Is it his son?"

"Yes, he tried to kill me because I wrecked their home. Sleeping with the boss has its consequences," states Natasha.

Allen jots down some notes and stares at Billy in deep thought. He motions to the officer and as he approaches he commands, "Take Billy to the station for questioning and wait for me there. Check with whoever has the authority to release him. If he is healthy enough to come in here to commit murder, he can come down to the station."

The officer releases Billy from his chair, gets him to his feet and places his hands behind his back to slap the cuffs on him. He pushes him toward the exit and out of the door. Natasha exhales a sigh of relief.

"Better?" asks Allen.

Natasha nods and smiles. The pain in her abdomen has completely subsided and with the absence of Billy she starts to relax. Allen, Natasha, Felicia, and another officer sit in silence for a moment until Felicia asks, "Would you like for me to check on Janet and send Landry in here with you?"

"Yes, I forgot she was here a while ago," Natasha replies as she squints her eyes.

Felicia grabs her small handbag as she is leaving the room. She opens it, looking through its contents while stating, "And, Detective Allen, I am licensed to carry, so it will be easy to search for me in the system." She pulls out her identification and permission to carry a weapon from her purse with an assured smirk at the corner of her mouth.

"Impressive," he says sarcastically. He continues, saying, "We are still going to the station for prints." Allen turns his attention back to Natasha and asks, "Is everything okay, Natasha?"

"Yes, Detective. My body is going through some changes and I feel a serious migraine coming on."

Clearing his throat, Detective Allen says, "Well, let's work as fast as possible, shall we? Start from the beginning of the night you were attacked."

It feels like Natasha is replaying days of information concerning that dreadful night. She can't help getting emotional when talking about the date with Jeff. Tears wash against her caramel cheeks as she brings the summary to a close and waits on her last line of questioning.

"Are you sure there isn't anything you left out? Even if it didn't seem important then, it could be important now," presses Detective Allen.

"Before I fell asleep today I received a call from Bruce and Bruce Junior wanting to talk about the events."

"They called you here?"

"Yes, sir. Mr. Wilson wanted me to be lenient on his son, to show a bit of sympathy. When I gave him my ass to kiss... sorry, butt... I got Side Show Bob in here, ready to open fire."

Landry had gotten comfortable at the foot of Natasha's bed about midway through her summary. She was able to hear about their first kiss, and Natasha having a real date. Her cousin attending Bible study was too much to process for the moment. She let it settle in her mind that Jeffery was good for her. Landry can also tell that Natasha loves him. Now, that's something she thought would never happen. Natasha in love.

"Miss Billingsworth, we are going to dump the phone lines and see where the calls came from. Maybe they were dumb enough to call from their personal numbers. There wasn't anyone that saw him enter or exit your place. Had it not been for the partial boot print on your abdomen we would have just concluded that you had a lovers' quarrel and decided to shoot Jeffery."

Natasha can feel the temperature rise in her cheeks as the rage within her reaches new heights. She bluntly comments in question form, "So, you're telling me that there isn't anything that points Bruce Junior to the crime, and it looks like Jeff and I were in a terrible fight? Are you shitting me, Detective?"

Surprised by her outburst and flared nostrils, Detective Allen is stunned. He closes his pad and places it into his pocket. Standing to leave the room he looks at Natasha and states, "That's exactly what I'm telling you. If this guy wasn't here to shoot you today, the jury would be putting nails in your coffin and ready to give you some jail time for shooting your lover. That's just what the scene looks like, Natasha."

CHAPTER TWENTY-EIGHT

The sound of nurses' sneakers, visiting family members and the "ding" from the elevator are all Natasha hears for the remainder of the day. After her choice words with Detective Allen, her mind had begun to hurt just as much as her heart. She thinks about Jeffery and his condition. Natasha blames herself for the things that have transpired. She can't comprehend how Bernadean Pattman can have such hope. At first, she couldn't even recognize him when she looked upon him lying in the hospital bed with all those bandages and the tubing that attached him to the machines. Yet Bernadean's face shined with the confidence that she knew her son would survive and be just fine. An hour passes before Natasha is able to break her thoughts.

As soon as her mind becomes quiet, there is stillness within the room, a peaceful silence that Natasha has grown to be comforted with. The Lord speaks, saying, "Did you really mean it when you cried in repentance?"

Natasha replies, "Yes, God, with all my heart."

"Then why do you continue to remind Me of what I have forgiven you for?" God questions, already knowing the answer.

"I feel great guilt for what I have done, and Jeffery is still critical, and many families are still ruined. I am the creator of this mess."

God informs her, "Bernadean has confidence in Me because I have never left her. She has battled sickness unto death, trouble in childbirth with Jeffery, and the loss of her family. In all this, she knows I am near and will keep her in My safety."

"She and I are two different people. Mrs. Pattman has probably known You longer than me."

"What is time to Me? I am time. I did these things for Bernadean before she confessed My Son. I set her family to pray for her generations before she was a thought to her parents. Before people are born naturally, you dwell here with Me. I appoint a time and place for you to dwell within the earth, for My works. That is recorded in Jeremiah chapter one verse five."

Natasha looks around for a Bible. She has enough common sense to know that God's reference was somewhere in the Bible. Her bedside tables have flowers on them covering most of the tops. She looks to her right and to her left several times and opens the drawers with great caution. With no luck in finding the Good Book, she sighs and gives up on her search. Laying her head back on her pillows, she hears the command, "Get the book out of the right beside table."

Leaning over slowly, she pulls open the drawer that was once filled only with her letters from Jeffery. Blinking twice, Natasha reaches in and pulls out the Bible, smelling new with the appearance of being untouched. She can't believe it. Holding it to her chest, she begins to cry because she can't believe her eyes and the contents she has in her hands.

God speaks, saying, "I have used your friends and family to soften your heart to receive Me, and also to warn you of your destruction. Read daily to build your strength so that you may not return to be the person you were. I have work for you to do."

"Thank You for knowing me and saving me. I can never repay You."

God states, "If this is the appreciation for what little you know about Me, wait until you get to know My love and what I have sacrificed for you. A song will be on your lips and in your heart praising My name for the rest of your life."

The peace lifts, leaving Natasha to her thoughts of the number of people who have had these experiences with God. Once, her perception of a higher power didn't exist. Even after all the talks from her friends and Landry. Natasha never thought about whether there was a God. She thought that if a god existed, it could and would not allow terrible things to happen to little girls; people wouldn't kill people, and married people would not go outside of their marriage for comfort.

Now, Natasha knows there is a God. She knows Jesus died for her sins, which were many, but it is okay because He has taken care of them. For once in her life, Natasha is grateful to have life and she wants to live this time the right way — right for her son and right for her soul, because now she believes she has one.

There is a light knock on her door, which startles Natasha a little. After the insane morning — and months, for that matter — Natasha has been unable to completely settle down. A little timid to say, "Come in," Natasha replies, "Acknowledge yourself."

The door is cracked just so the voice can be heard clearly. Landry stands on the other side of the door and responds by saying, "Should I come back later?"

"No, Dry Greens, come in here."

Natasha is happy that it is her favorite cousin and if she could she would give her the biggest hug she has in her. They air kiss then Landry pats Natasha's head and sits in the chair that is between Natasha and the exit where Detective Allen had sat previously.

"I would ask how you are, but it is obvious," states Landry.

"This makes you uncomfortable? Don't worry about saying the wrong thing. After these two days and especially this morning, I doubt anything would hurt my feelings."

Landry takes a deep breath and says, "I'm just happy you are alive. Your mom had to call a cleaning crew to straighten up your place but it is as good as new."

"I haven't even thought about home. Jeffery is still critical and only God and his mom knows how that's going to turn out."

The shock on Landry's face is very apparent when Natasha mentions God. A little boost in the eyes indicates she had received the information that Natasha has met his mother.

"So, when did you and God have a conversation? We can guess how you met his mother. I assume you went to see him today and ran into her. No brainer, but I know you didn't bump into God in the elevator on the way there," Landry concludes.

"This is going to sound crazy, but my attacker led me in the sinner's prayer. With all the fear and anger in me at that point, I still meant it when I prayed for Jesus to be my savior."

"That's deep," Landry replies with a puzzled look on her face.

"I'm just thankful that God's love runs deep enough even for me."

There is a brief silence before either of them speaks. Natasha has the memory about the girl trapped in a basement of some sort, and the place looks like Milan. She isn't sure if it is the meds or just her being paranoid, but she knows Landry is the person she can talk to about it.

"I had a nightmare, but I was awake – a vision, if you will. This wasn't my actual life, which is horrific in itself; I was really dreaming. The place looked like Milan because of the architecture and there was this big sign broadcasting Fashion Week. I was then in a dark place and could hear a girl whimpering. There were footsteps above my head so I knew we were in a low place like a basement. There were no lights in the place; it was pitch-black. I heard the footsteps coming down a set of stairs getting closer and closer. The girl's crying got more intense. I couldn't see her to get to her so I shushed her in hopes she would quiet down. Suddenly, there was silence, complete stillness, because the movement stopped. Bright lights shined through the door that had originally been closed. The girl let out a horrible scream and I woke up."

Landry sits there a minute processing the dream and the information it entailed. The location is odd because it is halfway around the world, and who is this crying person? Could God be trying to warn of future travels?

"Nat, I am supposed to go to Milan to showcase really soon. The line has taken off since Fashion Week here in New York. We have expanded and I have a crazy schedule. Do you think God is warning me of future dangers?"

"I don't know, maybe. You sitting in here with me right now is dangerous for the both of us and I haven't been awake more than seventy-two hours."

All Landry can do is take it as a sign. It is straightforward and Landry, out of everyone, believes in the truth of dreams and visions being a way God communicates with people. She had dreamt that her father would pass before he did and it was the same for sister-in-law. It gives her chills to think of herself being on the receiving end of danger and not just her cousin.

"I am going to pray about it, because I will have to pretend that there is an emergency — which there is — and send an assistant in my place. This would give me a much-needed rest."

"How is Janet?" Natasha inquires.

Landry begins to laugh and then replies, "She was so pissed off she was shot. Janet was speaking Spanish and being difficult. They gave her something for the pain and she's been asleep since. It just grazed her enough to leave a scar. I pray the person's strength that's going to be there when she wakes up."

"I missed you, Dry Greens."

"I missed you, Nat. To be honest, I didn't know if I could see you because I had mixed emotions about what happened. I felt bad in feeling like you brought this on yourself, but the other part of me knows no one deserves to be hunted down like an animal."

Natasha smiles a big smile at her favorite cousin and laughs a little. She takes in what her cousin just said and realizes there are people that have seen the ordeal on the television after her father's death. When they addressed her father's transgressions, they followed up with her dirty laundry. The mirror of her faults was large and heavy. Natasha is laughing because she feels that in this place she is in now, God will clear her reflection.

"There was a time when I would roll my eyes and give you plenty of attitude, but today I have to accept what I did and take ownership in cleaning what I can. The rest will just have to be taken care of by God."

"You are sounding a little deep. This, my dear, will take some getting used to."

"How is everything with you? You expanded the company? That's amazing!"

"It is so unreal. Everything is moving so fast, I can't take it all in. Not so long ago, I was begging for meetings with buyers and investors, now everyone is calling me. Amazing! I have to say, though, I am very afraid. Failure and I are not good friends."

With the look of a mother hen, Natasha is a little disappointed in her cousin's comment. She replies, "Are you not obtaining? Is everything not in motion? Take it in, because life is not promised, nor is having a successful business."

Landry sits back in her chair relaxed, taking a deep breath and letting her head rest on the back of the chair. She allows herself, just for a moment, to think on her gratefulness. Not her schedule, not her tiredness, but just on the fact she is right where she has wanted to be. A smile starts to part her lips and before she knows it, she is laughing. Landry laughs herself to tears as joy begins to bubble over from the feeling of success. Looking on with a big smile and giggles in agreement, Natasha is proud of her baby cousin, and takes this moment between them as treasure.

CHAPTER TWENTY-NINE

Waking from sleep, Natasha doesn't realize she had even dozed off. She turns to her right and the clock reads 3:25 a.m. She can't remember the time she fell asleep to calculate how many hours she has slept. Natasha doesn't feel like she got enough rest, though she thinks the coma should have been enough sleep for the rest of her life. The hospital was still, with the exception of the humming of generators. Taking a moment to reflect on yesterday's events, she rubs her belly, shaking her head. "Little one, I do not know what the future holds, but I will do my best to give what I can give you. That's all I can offer. Let's pray we make it out of this alive."

Remembering for a moment the chapter in the Bible the Lord spoke of, Natasha grabs the book. It takes her a moment to find the place because it takes that long to grasp the layout. She starts reading aloud to herself and her unborn, saying, "Before I formed you in the womb I knew you; before you were born I sanctified you; I ordained you a prophet to the nations."

After an hour and a half Natasha completes reading the book of Jeremiah the Prophet. She closes the Bible and is puzzled and saddened. He couldn't marry, couldn't live the way he wanted, and was always in someone's pit. All because he said what God wanted him to say to people. "His life was rough. Jesus, that must have been a struggle, and here I am creating my own heartache. He just did what You asked and look what it got him."

"He received a place with Me because of his obedience — the reward all receive who seek salvation and who accept the gift."

God speaking takes Natasha by surprise because the atmosphere usually changes before God talks. She takes it in stride due to the fact things are already quiet and calm. Natasha has learned to become more careful with her thoughts these days. She isn't really sure when God will start talking, and wonders if He ever runs out of things to say.

"I enjoy this time because men are resting upon their beds. This is the time man doesn't battle with Me and My will. I communicate in this hour, giving direction and instruction. It is easier when the person you are talking to is only on the receiving end. I have talked with you for years, but now you want to hear Me."

"I feel like I will continue to be Your student for the rest of my life and in the next. Please protect my loved ones. Please heal Jeffery and help his family to cope. God, protect Landry and continue to be with her. Be with Ashley, heal Janet, and the rest of my family needs You. Help those who are like me and didn't want to know You. Help them to want to know You and be with them, too. Amen." Her last word is barely off her lips as she dozes off into a peaceful sleep.

Bev is doing her morning rounds when she notices a figure enter Natasha's room. It is 8:30 in the morning, which is the time she normally pokes her head in to check for vital signs. Having a flashback of the recent events, she goes back to the nurses' station to get someone else to follow her into the room. The only available backup is a young twenty-something with the signature still wet on her diploma.

The two of them walk the fifteen feet to Natasha's room. Bev places her finger against her mouth so the other nurse knows not to make a sound. Bev counts down, three-two-one with the same hand. As soon as her index finger makes a fist, the two of them burst into the room to find Bernadean Pattman standing at the foot of Natasha's bed. She is startled by the sudden rush of guests. Her hand quickly finds her heart as she inhales enough breath for two people.

"What are you doing?" asks Bev with authority, as if she were a mother hen. Natasha is still asleep through the ordeal. Bev's accomplice is hanging close behind Bev as the women exchange words.

"I'm Jeff's mother. I decided to stop in and pray for Natasha before I went to see my son. No weapons drawn, honey, and I don't even have a purse."

Bernadean says her piece with such ease and charm that Bev decides she isn't a threat, but as a precaution Bev adds, "We can all pray with you."

The new nurse looks surprised and asks, "We?"

As the new nurse backs away, Bev and Bernadean look at her until she clarifies why she questioned. The new nurse speaks, "I do not know what you are praying to so you can count me out. I will be outside if you need me."

The morning is still a little quiet and there is a little buzz beginning to sound as the day is getting underway. The elevator begins to chime more often and there is the sound of toilets flushing along with doors closing, but Bernadean takes the time to speak with the nurse. She begins by saying, "Do you know who God is, child?"

"Not one specifically, but several gods."

"The God we are about to pray to is the Creator of all things, from the sand in the sea to the stars in the sky. He is the One that held you in His bosom and destined the number of hairs on your head and the color of your eyes way before your parents even existed. He is the all-knowing and all-seeing God above all gods," says Bernadean in a teacher's tone with soft eyes.

"Okay, so why place us in this crazy world if we were already at peace? Why allow death and deformities among people?"

Bernadean sighs and asks, "Do you believe in the devil? Do you believe that a battle can occur between good and evil?"

The young nurse bites her lip as she contemplates her answer. "I believe that there is a fight between good and evil. We see it every day. Bad people do bad things and the police try to catch them. There are always bad people and the good people try to do away with what's bad," she replies.

"Well, the devil was one of God's angels before the creation of man. But like bad people, there was something in him that wasn't right. He wanted to be God so he made a plan to overthrow Him and take His place. God, being all-knowing, could see what was happening. The devil gathered many followers but before he could make an attempt to do anything in heaven, God put him and his followers out with a mighty force. It appeared to be as lightning on the earth. Earth is where the devil is bound until the Son of God comes again."

"God has a Son?"

"Yes, my dear. His name is Jesus and He is the sole rightful heir to the throne of heaven. Over two thousand years ago, the earth was becoming more and more wicked. So God prepared a place for the devil and his followers called hell. People upon the earth were doing things just as evil as the devil because he was enticing them to do wrong. God noticed that the people, His children may not return to Him after their time on earth because all they saw was wickedness. So to redeem us, God prepared the most holy sacrifice He could that would wash all of our wickedness and sin away. Jesus, God's own Son, was crucified and died only to give man the opportunity to choose eternal life over damnation. The gift of life is a choice we have to choose on our own. Through Jesus we can live eternally. All we have to do is believe and live as He has taught us."

"It is hard to be a goody two shoes. There is no fun in that."

The two older ladies laugh as if they have heard the same joke before. Bev completes the explanation by saying, "That's why we pray. God has to work out of us the things that are too hard, and He has to teach us the way."

The new nurse is bobbing her head as if she is listening to her favorite song. She is taking everything that has been said into consideration and her heart is pricked by the fact that a God that knows everything knew that man wouldn't go to heaven and He gave up His only child. He was crucified and died so that we could have a choice regarding whether we wanted to go to heaven or we wanted to go to hell. The new nurse concludes, "I want to live. So what do I do?"

Bev and Bernadean are bubbling over with excitement as if they have just won the lottery. Bernadean informs her, "All you need is faith. Do you believe Jesus is the Son of God?"

"Yes. I believe Jesus is the Son of God," the new nurse confirms.

Then Bernadean asks, "Do you believe that Jesus was sent from heaven to die for the sins of the world so that we could live in eternity with the God Almighty?"

"Yes," she confirms once again.

By this time, the three have formed a circle and are facing one another by the entrance to Natasha's room. Bernadean is looking directly at the nurse as she says, "Repeat after me. Father of Jesus, Lord my Savior."

"Father of Jesus, Lord my Savior."

Bernadean continues, "I believe You are the Son of God who died for my sins…"

The nurse repeats, "I believe You are the Son of God who died for my sins…"

"And rose again with all power and victory in Your hands…" Bernadean states.

"And rose again with all power and victory in Your hands…"

Bernadean continues, "So that my life will be in Your hands and so that I will be Your servant forever."

"So that my life will be in Your hands and so that I will be Your servant forever."

"I believe that You are the true and living God, and the only God that keeps my soul," adds Bernadean.

"I believe that You are the true and living God, and the only God that keeps my soul."

Finishing, Bernadean states, "Thank You, Jesus, for washing away my sins and making me eligible to enter Your kingdom. Thank You for forgiving me and receiving me."

The new nurse is crying and speaking with her eyes closed, "Thank You, Jesus, for washing away my sins and making me eligible to enter Your kingdom. Thank You for forgiving me and receiving me into Your bosom once again."

"Amen," finishes Bernadean. Then they all say, "Amen."

The women are giggling like little school girls sharing the story behind their first kiss. Natasha begins to turn in her sleep, and Bernadean realizes she has gotten side-tracked in a great way. She says, "Now that God has one of His little angels back and the rest of them are dancing in heaven over this moment, let's pray for Natasha."

Bernadean walks over to her bed and grabs hold of Natasha's feet. Bev walks over and places her hand on Bernadean's right shoulder, and the new nurse follows and places her hand on the left shoulder. There is stillness in the room that is noticeable to the new nurse. She doesn't let it faze her because the other two continue like it is another day's work.

Bernadean begins praying for Natasha, but her prayer isn't as sweet and easy like it was with the new nurse being ushered into the kingdom. This prayer is of someone who has knowledge of God and how to go right up to His door, knowing they are going to get in. The new nurse looks in amazement at the transformation that has taken place, even in her tone of voice. Bernadean is saying words like "bind," "loose," "curse," and "full armor of God." That is all the new nurse understands before she starts talking in another language. It is strange that she didn't pick up on an accent while they were talking, but what Bernadean is speaking now is by no means English. Bev starts speaking in a low tone that sounds like a mumble. The only thing the new nurse understands is, "Thank You, Jesus."

The three words begin to be a chant as they flow off the new nurse's tongue. There is an intense pressure in the room, yet it isn't threatening. All of a sudden, the new nurse hears Bev say, "If you want the gift of the Holy Ghost, you better ask now while the opportunity is here."

The new nurse isn't sure what the Holy Ghost is exactly, but if God is giving something out she wants it. She says within herself, "May I have the Holy Ghost, please?" She continues her chant for a few more moments and her tongue feels as if someone is moving it about inside her mouth. The new nurse begins to speak in other tongues just as Bernadean is doing. She feels a fire begin to kindle within her belly and joy like nothing she has ever experienced all at the same time. There is such laughter within her she can hardly stand it. The new nurse begins to dance and praise God uncontrollably. As the spirit of God begins to ascend the women look at one another and begin to giggle once again. The new nurse is wiping the tears from her eyes with a beam of excitement on her face.

Natasha is still asleep, to everyone's surprise. Fifteen minutes have passed since Bev and the new nurse entered the room. Bev looks at her watch and says, "The Word of God is quick."

"Powerful and sharper than any two-edged sword," completes Bernadean. She continues, saying, "Today is a great day. Now, you must pray every day with your new prayer language. Your language changed in your sight to prove that the Spirit of God lives within you. If a person doesn't accept Jesus into their heart they're not qualified to receive the gift of the Holy Ghost. This is done so that you would know that Jesus still sits at the right hand of God."

"I can't wait to tell everyone I know how Jesus is real," says the new nurse with excitement and joy.

As the three are leaving the room, the new nurse exits first with a bounce in her step, greeting everyone that passes her in the hallway. Bev pulls Bernadean back a step by grabbing her arm gently. She wants to inquire about something she said while she was praying. Bev asks, "Did God say something to you about Natasha having a miscarriage?"

Bernadean looks back at Natasha and then back at Bev with a sadness in her eyes. "Yes, He did. God knew that the baby wouldn't complete his destiny at this appointed time. So He is going to keep him for a little while longer."

Bev knows that good news is the gospel of Christ. However, news that informs of a situation before it happens can spark tons of emotions within a person. Natasha is a strong woman, and Bev has no doubt she will pull through this just as she has done everything else that has transpired.

CHAPTER THIRTY

The heavy eyes of Jeffery Pattman open suddenly due to a feeling that he isn't alone. His sight is all he has. Jeffery couldn't acknowledge Natasha when she entered the room, nor could he react after she was startled. He felt less than a man because he couldn't be there for her, do anything for her, or protect her. The weight of the burden he carries as her protector has become heavy, knowing he hasn't fulfilled his duty in that position. Jeffery looks toward the window in hopes of seeing if he can guess what time of day it is.

Surprising to his line of vision is a very well-dressed man sitting in the chair next to his bed looking upon him intently. As if waiting on him to awaken. Jeffery can't tell the man's nationality, nor can he identify the color of his eyes, the shape of his nose, or his hair color. Things are worse than he thought.

"Don't be frightened, Jeff. I do not come to cause harm."

Jeffery guesses that the man had seen his name on the charts located somewhere in the room. He is dressed as if going to a formal affair. The suit is tailored to perfection like nothing Jeffery has ever seen; the fabric itself is of high quality. Jeffery can't help but enquire, "Who are you?"

The man chuckles as if Jeffery has told a joke and answers, "You have called on Me all your life. Now that we have business and I show up, you ask My identity? I should be asking who you are. There are so many tubes and bandages I really can't tell."

The man laughs some while leaning in closer to Jeffery with His left elbow on His knee and His right arm bent to where His hand is placed on His right knee. Confused at where this conversation is going, Jeffery decides to ask a safe question.

"What business do we have together?"

He answered, "Well, I have to tell you that you are finally right where I want you, still enough to hear Me. Busy, busy, busy, Mr. Pattman. I will do a thing to prove you and I have met, and to increase your faith. But before I do, you need to be My mouthpiece. Others, like you, are too busy to listen. Your boss, the one you won the big case for, is first on the list. Tell him that I said he is guilty. He is guilty in his marriage, in his business, and in that thing he thought I didn't see on his father's bed when he was seventeen. He has a short season to repent. Very short, or the wrath of God will be the repercussion."

There is a pause. Jeffery has to process all that is being said. After being sure of what he has heard, he internally thinks, Continue. The Holy Ghost goes on to say, "Second, Ashley hasn't taken care of herself in the way she should since she received the verdict that she would never bear children. Tell her to care for herself the way her husband met her and the fire will be back in her marriage. I give the last say, not man."

Thinking on how to tell his cousin something so personal is deeper than him calling out his boss for his wrongdoing. He figures if God puts him in charge of doing this business, then there is no need to doubt whether she will receive it or not.

"Lastly, Natasha is a piece of work, but she is your wife, and she will do great things in My name, and she will be a rock for you. Where I am going to take you, you're going to need a companion. I send them out by two, you know? Tell her to be strong, because she will bear children, just not now."

Jeffery is surprised and thrilled because in the midst of the conversation he realizes that it is God he is speaking with. All of the stories he heard growing up could not compare to what is taking place right now. At this very moment, God is more real to him than ever before. It was always his mother that spoke of times of hardship and professed that God made a way, but there is nothing like firsthand experience. Jeffery knows that he knows God is alive, and a great dresser, too! Worried he will fail at his tasks, he asks, "What if I forget what You have told me to say, Lord?"

Immediately Jeffery feels his face tingle, and as God stands he notices that he can follow His moves because his head is moving. "Look upon yourself," commands the Spirit of God. He gives himself the once-over. There are no bandages or tubing, and the machinery doesn't beep. Jeffery touches his arms, legs, chest, and face. He is glad that he can feel the sensation of touch. The only thing standing in the way of him leaving the hospital that instant is the hideous gown he is wearing. As the Spirit of God stands at the foot of his bed, He states, "This time tomorrow, you would have made a miraculous recovery, and the first order of business will be for you to tell Natasha everything you've experienced."

In the blink of an eye, He is gone. There isn't a remnant that someone else was in the room prior to the nurse's arrival. Just Jeff, the tubing, loud beeping, and that ugly gown, but within, he is praising God. Once again unable to speak, he is aware that his rapid eye movement and occasional blinks are noticed by the nurse. Tears are streaming from his eyes, and when he opens them she can tell he is smiling from within. "I'm glad to see another day too, Mr. Pattman," she addresses him, and starts humming as she makes her way around, checking his vitals.

***

In Michelle's kitchen stand Tessa, Nathanel, Janet, and Michelle. They are having breakfast and laughing about childhood stories about the children they have raised. Nathanel is beet-red and keeps his hands over his face most of the time Tessa is speaking because the most outlandish stories are about him. There is a pause in the laughter and reality soon sets in to Janet's mind. She asks, "Why is it that Natasha has never spoken of her childhood? I have been friends with her for years and there has never been a crazy story of harsh punishments."

Michelle takes a deep breath and answers, "After Nat reached a certain age she stopped talking to me so much, ya know? It was like a barrier was put up between me and my own child — a big one. I didn't know how to reach her and her dad was away so much that when he was home it was like a picnic. It wasn't until before Bryant passed that we all learned that she was raped by the men I was having affairs with. Drunken nights of me trying to fill the loneliness had my daughter in torture for years. She kept it all to herself, never telling anyone until we went and met Tessa and the boys for the first time."

Tessa places one hand on top of Michelle's and uses the other to wipe a tear from her eye and states, "It is unfair that in an instant, a parent who makes a mistake can lose their child. In this case, we are lucky Natasha is still alive, and her child, too, after all the chaos that started with us. We are apparently not the Brady Bunch."

"Everything is just starting to make sense. It is like you see your friend who you love on a path that will lead to destruction. Your love and honesty is all you can give, but when that isn't enough you feel like you have failed and let that person down. Seeing her in a coma was the hardest thing, but I was happy that she was breathing because I knew there would be some hope that she could still pull through and live," says Janet.

Nathanel puts his arm around Janet as they continue to sit at the island in silence for a moment. Their relationship has started to blossom more and more each day. It is new, and Nathanel is such an understanding person that it is beyond Janet's comprehension. Janet cannot fight the feeling that the relationship isn't going to last much longer. She is hoping this feeling is wrong, but she can't shake it. Something is going to happen and they will part ways. Janet is just hoping that whatever happens, the family doesn't change the way they see her or feel awkward when the two of them are around each other for Natasha's sake.

CHAPTER THIRTY-ONE

The office of the late Bryant Billingsworth is still just as lively and thriving at the same capacity as it had before his death and scandals. Bryant Junior had been taught very well about the operations, processes, and procedures of the company. Shadowing his father over the years had better prepared him for his new role. Bryant had been more than happy to have a predecessor to take over the company. He had never been comfortable about leaving the business to strangers, so in hindsight his affair had led to another great business decision.

The first weeks at the office there was plenty of furniture being rearranged concerning people and policies. This ruffled plenty of feathers with the investors, stakeholders, and tenured employees. The change was for the better and for the furtherance of the company. Some areas were stagnating in growth and Bryant Junior had just the plan to change that.

As he looks out of his office window he can see the setting of the Manhattan sun. Bryant Junior loves his career. He had prayed that his father would see that he was business-savvy and place him in charge when the time came. The time came sooner than he had hoped. His father's office is now his. He has kept his father's desk and chair and promises he will remove certain items little by little. That is how he grieves. Like his father, he doesn't cry that much.

Bryant Junior likes to think about the good memories. He had a knowing when he was a child that his father wasn't typical and that they were not like most families of his class. It was strange to lie in most cases and say that his father was a traveling big shot who spent most of his time in New York City working. It surprised him that Mr. Bryant Billingsworth had managed to make it to almost everything important in his childhood.

There were his own softball and chess tournaments and basketball games, and Nathanel participating in everything art would have left a father with only one family sick with busyness. Bryant Billingsworth had two families. Bryant Junior remembered his father talking about Natasha and all of her accomplishments and activities. He always thought of her as Tinkerbell, who was in a land far away. He knew one day they would meet, but not like this.

It is only natural for children in this situation to feel angry or hurt. Nathanel has always been a little more on the emotional side. He would confront his father directly and get everything his soft heart had on it off. One confrontation had ended with Nathanel connecting a right hook to Mr. Billingsworth's left jaw.

Conversely, Bryant Junior liked an indirect approach like putting liquid laxatives in his dad's Scotch, or hiding his important work papers so that he couldn't leave when he planned. The biggest thing he did was call Mr. Billingsworth's home. Unlike busy Dad, the other two were home. "Hey, Dad! When are you coming home?" asked a ten-year-old Natasha. Stunned that he had actually heard her voice for the first time ever, he was speechless. He already had a hard time accepting his life's truth but this just solidified that it was a reality. His mother was in a relationship with someone who had a family, and that someone was his father.

"Mr. Billingsworth, I am very sorry to bother you, but we are already ten minutes late for your meeting. I sent the flowers to your sister as you requested," informs his assistant. Bryant Junior turns to look at the person who was with his father for thirty-five years. He can't help but wonder what she knew then and how she thought of his family.

Placing his hands into his pants pockets, he rocks once on the balls of his feet and asks, "What did you really think of our family? My mom working here, and me shadowing my father knowing there would be a possibility I would take over the family business. We were not the model bunch."

"Mr. Billingsworth, I am not the one to judge, nor am I the person whose opinion is highly valued, but I loved Mr. Billingsworth and both his families. Never agreed with his affair and the choices he made to keep you kids separate." She comes into the room and closes the door behind her as she speaks. "It was hard keeping you hidden when Michelle popped up. I can't tell you how your mother cried every time she was downplayed as just another employee. Those moments I wish I could forget. My heart is happy knowing that the secret's out and that all is on the table. It has been a long time coming. I worry most about you, though."

Bryant Junior cocks his head to the side in surprise and asks, "Why?"

The assistant walks closer to him. Places the files in her hand on the desk and stands toe-to-toe. "You are just like your father. Your mannerism, your attitude, being driven to succeed. I pray for your happiness, that instead of trying to become or be greater than your father, you search your life and really find what makes you happy. Can you promise me that?"

"I do not make promises. But I definitely can say I will take more vacations."

She laughs and says, "Well, that's a big start."

The assistant picks up the files and heads for the exit, calling over her shoulder, "You are really late, remember?"

Bryant Junior remembers the assistant very well. Whenever Mr. Billingsworth got a call of urgency she would be the first person to be summoned to take him the play room they had in the office building. When he became a teen he felt it was a little ridiculous to be told to make a coffee run when they had plenty at the office. He said nothing, just found something to do with himself. To his surprise, when he saw Michelle Billingsworth for the first time in his mother's foyer, he didn't recognize her. The day he saw her it was a relief, because he could now be himself, instead of the best known secret at the office.

CHAPTER THIRTY-TWO

Nerge has seen better days than today, but Melvin Junior couldn't ask for more. Well, he could, but it wouldn't arrive in the next twenty minutes. He is down a short-order cook, two waitresses and a hostess, and open for business. He is finally through the lunch rush and is turning things over for dinner. He wants so much to close up the restaurant and get home to his children, a tank top, and a cold beer.

Melvin feels like the worst cousin because he can't get to see Natasha at the hospital. He would send the kids on Sundays when Michelle would go. His daughter would report on how many times Natasha's eyes would flicker and if her leg jumped. Sometimes she would pass gas and the little girl would laugh about that for a week.

The second Melvin had to fantasize about what he wanted to do, reality became a little more difficult. Passing by the front window is a couple intensely gazing into each other's eyes and caressing each other's hands. His view is soon occupied by the city inspector. This takes about an hour and forty minutes of time he doesn't have. This day just keeps getting better, he thinks.

On the other side of Manhattan is Detective Allen, trying to put the pieces together. The accusation Natasha made against Bruce Wilson Junior had him unconvinced. She could be upset that the affair is over and being publicized. Now, she can no longer frame him. He is eating a Baconator while doing some digging at the office into the boy's history. The more he looks the more shade he uncovers.

Bruce Wilson has used most of his fortune in legal fees to keep his son from going to prison for some of the crimes he has committed. The dark secrets started when he was only a child stealing the pets of their neighbors, with their owners never seeing them again. His crimes escalated as he became a teen... to assault. A childhood friend was at his home when they had a disagreement that ended with Bruce Junior strangling the girl unconscious and hiding her in his closet. The girl's family pressed charges but the high-paid lawyer got him off with the condition of intense therapy. The list continued with several fights at school, no work history, and other misdemeanors that his father kept bailing him out of.

This kid is barely in his twenties and has seen the inside of a courtroom more times than a student trying to pass the bar. Bruce Junior is smart and with the financial backing of his father he can do whatever he wants.

Detective Allen grabs his jacket from the hook by the exit, whistles for a ride-along and heads to the residence of the Wilsons. It is before rush hour in the afternoon so it won't take them long to reach Fifteenth Street.

CHAPTER THIRTY-THREE

Landry pricks herself for the third time as she is completing the hem on one of her favorite pieces for Fashion Week in Milan. She can't help having the shakes after visiting Natasha at the hospital the week before. In about four days she will be in beautiful Italy with fabulous clothing and other top designers. She hopes she won't become stricken by shock after seeing some of the most iconic people present their lines in their shows, as well.

Landry's first showing is early in the day and she is afraid no one will show up. Now, she can't have a moment in the workday without someone calling her name or needing to fix a problem. If this is what success is going to be like from here on out, Landry feels as if she could deal. Of course, there are some things to be added to her checklist. On her list are children, husband, and vacations, but not in that order. She feels as if everything is progressing smoothly, yet still bumpy enough to be exciting.

As she works in her loft space at the same window where Natasha had a panic attack months prior, she ponders what her significant other will look like, and even what their children will look like. Will they be sun-kissed with untamed hair? Is their father going to be tall, round or hairy? This guessing game makes her giggle.

Her assistant is buzzing around the office along with two other workers on this rainy Tuesday trying to piece together last-minute looks to be boxed, shipped and made ready for Milan. Landry likes the fact that she can ignore the phone, doorbell, and people if the problem can be handled by her staff.

Staff. Now there's another thing Landry didn't think would come so quickly. That thought makes her giggle a little more.

Unknown to her, there is a buzz at the door along with an announcement that there's a package she has to sign for. Her assistant has to get directly in front of the bust form in order for her to come out of the cloud of bliss in which she had enveloped herself. "There is a package that requires a signature," says her assistant. Landry finds this mighty strange, because the assistant would usually have taken care of the matter quickly and without her help.

Landry starts to get annoyed and follows the assistant to the lobby of the office, preaching about the employees having the authority to do almost everything she can do, when the sight of the delivery man seals her lips. He isn't so muscular that it is overbearing. He isn't so short that he can't make her feel safe. She knows exactly how Goldilocks felt when trying out the food and beds… he is just right.

Her assistant is leading the way, saying, "The person in charge must sign for all packages, and this one is a special delivery, so you must sign."

"Special indeed," says Landry before she can even think it. The delivery guy smiles and apologizes about coming in wet, because he got caught in the rain and the package requires a signature.

"It's okay. We are all made of mostly water." She really doesn't know where to go from there.

Almost being forward, she is going to ask him out but he says, "Have you been in business long? It's not that often my station drops at this building."

"Your station?"

He replies, "Yes, my name is Travis Rispit. I own the delivery hub for FedEx in this area. I don't recall a log for this location for special deliveries."

"We have been here for about a month. I was working out of my apartment with no assistant prior to this."

"Congratulations on progress." Travis is looking around at the workers that appear to be busy but anyone can tell they are eavesdropping."Everyone looks like they are preparing for something major."

"Yes, I have a clothing line and we are leaving for Fashion Week in Milan in three days. It is going to be lots of work, but a ton of fun."

"That sounds very exciting and I'm happy for you. It seems like things are taking off. This is my last stop for the day. If you don't mind, I would like to ask you to dinner tonight. Well, I see you are busy, so it is more like me going to get cleaned up and give you and the rest of your team a reason to take a break – good food."

Landry really doesn't want to shut him down, but the workaholic in her is screaming, "Put him out!" while the other side is saying, "Break time!" His puppy dog eyes are looking back at her with an endearing plea. Oh, how could she resist?

"Sounds good, but I have got to ask, do you ask out all the women you meet on special deliveries… and their entire staff?"

"No. I am never in the truck, but when your employee gets sick halfway through the shift and there's no one to cover, what do you do? I figured it's now or never, because as attractive as you are, and as beautiful as Milan is, you may never come back. Then I would have missed my opportunity. We don't even have to exchange numbers yet. That way you can still forget we met. What do you say, pizza joint on the corner in two hours?"

As Landry closes the door on the heels of Travis with a smile, she can't believe she has agreed to go out with a complete stranger who boldly asked her out in front of her employees and went so far as to offer to buy all of them dinner, right in the foyer of the place she now owns. She is impressed! She puts her nonchalant face back on and says, "Back to work, and quickly, because in two hours we may have an extended break."

"Jesus, You are quick!" Landry mumbles to herself as she heads back toward her incomplete hem. Package in hand, she finally looks down at the label. It is from Natasha. Surprised, she opens it immediately, because she had no idea anything was coming. Landry kicks herself because Natasha is getting out of the hospital in two days. Last she had heard, Jeffery was still critical.

The box has the contents that would equip any girl for travels. There are a few important things Landry always forgets when traveling – cash, hair products in travel size, toiletries, and a camera. Enclosed is a handwritten note,

Dry Greens,

I know you have worked hard toward your goal and you have finally done it! I am so proud of you words cannot express it. You are the woman every girl should look up to. I am your big cousin, but you are my example to follow. Not just in your

career but in the way you follow God and your heart. You are going to do great and be even greater.

I know my dream cautioned you and Jesus will protect you. Just in case you wanted more security, this is the guy I picked personally. Here is his card. Be safe, have fun and indulge in this moment because it is yours.

Love,
Nat

Landry is so taken by surprise and so touched by the words her cousin shared that she takes a moment to call her. It amazes her that after all Natasha has been through, she can still remember what is going on with others. Natasha had been this way even before the tragedy. This is why her friends have always stuck to her – because they all know there is some good in her.

Landry also lets out some details about her near-future dinner date. They squeal like school girls and hang up with the feeling that all will be okay.

CHAPTER THIRTY-FOUR

Is he the man of her dreams? Maybe.

Landry sits across from Travis Rispit, engulfed in the most intense conversation about life, politics, aspirations, and the people they admire the most. The two-hour break is continuing for these individuals who sent the employees back to complete the work thirty minutes earlier. They check the time and start out to follow in their footsteps to the office.

There is a light drizzle and it is approaching ten o'clock at night when they are passing loft number two on West Twenty-Sixth Street. Landry knows that there will be only five more lofts to go before they are at her studio and she doesn't want the conversation to end.

"When are you due back in the States?" inquires Travis. He is eager to see her again and is hoping that they can see where things could lead. She seems to be a workaholic and with his changing schedule, he really doesn't know when they are going to have time to get to know each other better.

"I will be back in a week. Hopefully, my cousin will be out of the hospital and everything will be more oiled in my business. The expansion is a new machine and I am trying not to let it get away from me."

They are at the entrance to her place. Each is timid about what to say to the other. This exchange between the two of them is so new and very much needed. Travis Rispit has seen his share of failed relationships and he has promised himself that when he gets another chance he isn't going to pick her… the same woman who is shallow, without any drive or a hint of compassion. Time past has shown that he isn't a great judge of character. There is something about the woman in the loft with the untamed mane that has sparked his curiosity.

So entranced are they with each other that they don't notice the van that is park at the doorway. If they were paying attention, they would see that it isn't unoccupied, due to the small heap of cigarette butts outside the driver's window. Normally, Landry has a nose for anything unhealthy, since she is so conscious about her wholesome living and eating right. Right now she is oblivious.

She has her back to the van facing the entrance, which is blocked by Travis' ruddy stature and his great smile. It isn't until his face turns to fright that the feeling of bliss suddenly dissipates. She feels a sudden force pull her backward. All she remembers is Travis reaching for her and then things suddenly go black. There is something over her face when the doors to the van slam shut. No one says a word except a raspy voice yelling, "Take care of him!"

Landry fights, but her hands are restrained quickly and uncomfortably. She screams while her mouth is being taped to make the bag over her head a semi-permanent covering. She tries to kick and in reward is tied like a hog headed off to the slaughter. Dry Greens is a tough nut and hard to crack, and never in her life has she felt terror. In this situation, however, she is full of fear and her thoughts are going a mile a minute, all in the direction of the worst possible outcome. Moments ago, she was fantasizing about Milan, Fashion Week and her future husband, who had appeared out of nowhere.

That bastard set me up, thinks Landry. Enraged, she begins to squirm and move about the back of the van that has no seats. She isn't alone in this section of the carriage. Suddenly she feels a knee in her back. That person is applying their bodyweight on her to keep her from moving. His breath is hot against her face through the covering. It isn't a foul odor, surprisingly. The smell is of a stick of Winterfresh gum. The person on her back informs her, "Like your cousin, you won't have much of a love life after I am done with you."

After what feels like an eternity of driving, the van comes to a sudden stop and she can hear the gear being shifted into park. She has lost count of the number of turns they made right or left. It seems a lot easier when spies do it on television. The only thing she has in mind at this very moment is to survive.

Landry thinks about Natasha's dream and how this would be happening in Milan if the warning had been for her. Milan is definitely out of the ordinary, but then again, so were the occurrences of the day. If the guy yelled to get rid of Travis, then either he is in on it and wants it to appear as if he has nothing to do with it, or he is in the gutter because he is a witness. Someone has been watching what Natasha and the people who are closest to her, and now doing everything for her. Who knows how long this goon has been waiting on a window of opportunity? He has finally gotten his chance, and Landry just might be damned.

She is carried into an unknown building by three men. They literally throw her into a dark, dank room after walking her downstairs. It is a few degrees cooler where they are so Landry knows she is by water. The air is crisp and moist, as if they are standing on a harbor or by a river.

The kidnapper walks over to her and cuts her free, but doesn't remove the tape or the hood from her face. He warns, "If you scream, no one will hear. If you beg, I do not care. Only God is going to get you out of this. If He doesn't see fit to save you, then you will starve and the rats will eat away at your slowly rotting flesh."

He cuts the tape from her face using a knife. She keeps very still so that she won't be wounded on account of her squirming. Landry believes he has every intention for her to stay there and rot. If there are rodents, she knows they will be attracted to the blood.

Her eyes adjust to the light in the basement and she can see her assailant, Bruce Junior, wild-eyed and excited over his current catch. Landry begins to back away from him. Swallowing hard, she notices his tight grip on the knife he has in his hand. A wall against her back lets her know there is no other place to go but forward. She closes her eyes and starts to pray. Her mouth is moving, but nothing comes out.

Looking upon this eclectic beauty, Bruce Junior is stunned. "Are you a believer? This is most refreshing," he states, as he can see her lips moving although no sound proceeds from them.

"I am," confirms Landry, never looking him in the face. She continues to pray as he looks on. The room begins to fade to nothing. His presence doesn't pose a threat. The calm that surrounds Landry is the peace she has always hoped to find on the other side; that is, if it is her fate to die right now, in this place. The peace surpasses her understanding. She repents of her sins and asks for the will of God to be done.

After her prayers are complete, she is relaxed and collected. With her eyes still closed, she leans her head against the wall behind her. Stretches out her legs in front of her and crosses her ankles. She intertwines her fingers and places them in her lap. Landry sits as if she is soaking in the ambiance of the Lord on a beach with a fruity drink next to her.

Perplexed, Bruce Junior remarks, "I'm guessing God has you covered. There would be nothing that I could do to you right now that would sway your confidence in Him. Like Daniel in the lion's den, huh?"

Landry says nothing. She relaxes in the presence of the Most High. There is no indication of what will happen next, nor does Landry care about the outcome at this very moment. She finally understands how people can say God is their peace. Everything is horrific around her, unknown, and here she is... chilling. Then God begins to speak, He doesn't do so verbally in audio in her ear, but she is aware that the Holy Spirit is putting things in her belly to say.

She begins, stating with no emotion, "'Thank you for bringing Natasha to Jesus and to Me,' says God. 'Now that her position in my kingdom is set, we need to look at yours. You have run terror in the land of your father and in your life. You use Me while doing your mischief, and yet you do not know Me yourself. Your hypocrisy will cost you your life in this world and the next. Your days are short on this earth, shorter than you arrogantly think. But, that can change if you are willing to change. You have to start now... today! Otherwise, you will be lost and I will no longer be able to help you,' says Jesus, your Light upon your pathway," closes Landry as her prophecy comes to an end.

CHAPTER THIRTY-FIVE

Nerge is still understaffed and Melvin can't get the trainees up to expert status fast enough. The phones are ringing off the hook even though it is a Tuesday. All the more reason for him to be glad to be in business. He is wearing different hats today. Right now he is a host and a server. In a few minutes, he will be on the grill to catch up the backup, and between that he will answer the phones.

As he buzzes past the phone that is closest to the checkout he grabs it, answers, and proceeds to calculate the check for the ticket that is in his hand. The trainee knows something is wrong. Melvin appears as if all of the blood has rushed from his face. Stunned, he places the phone on the receiver, returns to the table and hands the customer their ticket and card.

He returns to the cash station and pulls the microphone that is hooked to the sound system to his mouth. Pressing the intercom button, Melvin announces, "Could I please have your attention? I have a major family emergency. I thank you all for your patience with me and my team, but I am going to have to ask that you leave as quickly as possible." At this point, Melvin is in tears as he continues, "Do not worry about your bill, and for those of you who are waiting to be seated, and waiting for your food, please take a business card from the hostess to my right as you exit. The next meal is on me. Thank you for being understanding, and keep my family in your prayers."

The entire restaurant is staring in disbelief at the announcement that was just made, and so are his employees. Melvin hands the keys to the most tenured person on his staff and says, "You guys clean when everyone is out. Lock up and I will call you tomorrow to let you know if we will open." As he leaves the restaurant, he immediately dials Michelle back, because she was causing his pocket to vibrate as he was giving his exit speech. He leaves Nerge with the weight of the world on his shoulders.

***

Travis is rushed to Lenox Hill Hospital barely breathing and critical.

An hour had passed since the appointed time Landry said she would return. She is never late, so the assistant went looking for the new flame in suspicion, partially because she wanted to see if Landry was finally getting action at the entrance, and also because Landry is a stickler for time. After finding her Prince Charming badly beaten with a stab wound to the chest and tucked in some trash close to the building, she immediately called the police.

In case of emergency — if she becomes ill or goes missing, or if there is a fire or accident — Landry has trained everyone about what to do. It was like teaching a new fire drill when she came back from seeing Natasha. Everyone knew something was up, but never in a million years did they think they would have to put the plan into action.

First, the police were to be notified. Second, call next of kin, who is Melvin. And last, call Michelle, who is her aunt and the glue to the memory of her father.

After they complete all directed steps, the room is silent, overcome by the shock of what is happening. The workers, paid and unpaid, have big decisions to make. Without Landry spearheading the big event, travel plans, the lineup, models, and meetings with potential retailers, the team is at a standstill. All they can do is wait to see what will happen, and pray that Landry will be okay and in one piece.

CHAPTER THIRTY-SIX

There is so much Natasha is thankful for when she awakes Wednesday. Her doctor has given the okay for her to be released the following day; her baby is healthy even though she started spotting. This morning her ribs gave her only minor discomfort when she turned to get out of bed. She is feeling like her old self in a new way. All she can think about is what her new life is going to bring. Optimism is something she has never experienced and today she is full of it.

The feeling of euphoria radiates from Natasha. Earlier, the nurse had opened the curtains, so the sunshine is pouring in and Natasha welcomes the beams on her unmade face. She feels as if she is being kissed by God and enjoys every moment of it. A knock at the door interrupts her glee. When she turns, her mother and Melvin are standing in the room with faces of despair. Immediately, Natasha knows it is Landry. She begins to cry.

"No need for tears right now, Nat. We have to think so they can find her before she is dead," Michelle declared.

Natasha replies, "She's missing?"

"Yes. Her team called me last night after they discovered the guy that joined them on a break. He was found stabbed in the trash next to the stoop by her office. There was nothing but a pile of cigarette butts in the street where a car could have been waiting. No Landry," Melvin informs her.

He is angry. Melvin has the type of fury in his eyes that would tell anyone he isn't to be messed with. He has obviously had no sleep and is wearing the same clothes he had on the night before, stained with signs of him being at Nerge when he heard the news.

Natasha begins, "I had a dream that Landry would be abducted in Milan. I begged her not to go. Of course, she wasn't going to miss the chance of her life, but I never guessed she would be snatched here."

Coming in on the last sentence of the happenings is Bernadean Pattman, Jeffery's mother. She visits regularly in the morning and it is routine for her to check on Natasha between sittings with her son. "Morning. How are we today?" She chimes with a glittering smile on her face.

Michelle and Bernadean have become really familiar. Michelle informs her of what is going on and introduces her to her nephew in the process. After the introductions, Bernadean sits on the edge of the bed with Natasha and asks her to repeat what she walked in on. Natasha tells her the dream in detail and informs her that she had warned Landry not to go to Milan. She had been wrong, and her baby cousin was abducted right here at home.

Bernadean delves into her explanation by saying, "Dreams are not always cookie cutouts of exactly what is going to happen. You have to pray to get the whole story of what God is trying to reveal to you. Now, when you look at it, Fashion Week in Milan will be in full swing, but the person in your dreams is locked away. Landry is going to miss the fashion show, but she will be alive while it is going on, so there is still hope in finding her. You have to think very hard about where she was in the dream. Think about what you smelled. What you felt against your skin. Noises you may have heard. All of these things can be helpful in finding her."

Closing her eyes and laying her head back onto her pillow, Natasha thinks very hard about her dream. The lights were flashing from the fashion show but she couldn't focus on that because it was only the reference of time. She thought about where she was. She remembered there were stairs. Her thoughts bring her to the moisture in the room that made the air musty.

"Water! There must be water somewhere close by because the air was moist and I could hear metal clanking together, and the horns of ships not too far away. A shipyard, maybe," Natasha concludes. Her eyes spring open wider as her memory cranks into overdrive. She can remember conversations with Bruce about boats and shipping and how he liked to be on the water. She is sure he owns some property or even a boat himself, just for the joy of his pastime.

Detective Robert Allen enters the room and halts when he sees the mini crowd of people. "Well, at least there are no lunatics and no one is shot this time when I enter," he says sarcastically. "Michelle, I got the call. Landry is now missing?" he asks.

"Yes, she was taken from her studio around ten last night and no one has seen or heard from her. The gentleman that was walking her to the office is here with a stab wound to the chest and badly beaten, but he's going to make it."

Detective Allen takes a deep breath and says, "Are we going to conclude that little Bruce is at it again? We still can't get a handle on him. That's the thing about New York and the rich. They always have somewhere to hide, but they get reckless when they are arrogant and eventually get caught."

"Detective Allen, he could have Landry in a shipyard somewhere owned by his father. I am sure Daddy isn't going to give up his son willingly, so you may have to check his records," Natasha suggests.

"Wait, how do you know how she may be kept? Has anyone tried to contact you again?" inquires the detective.

"I had a dream about a girl being abducted. According to what I heard and felt in the dream, that is where she would be. It makes sense also, because Bruce may have property by a shipyard; he loves boats," Natasha concludes.

"You want me to do this investigation on the sole basis of something you dreamed? I didn't start on the force yesterday," snares Detective Allen.

Natasha snaps, saying, "My cousin is missing and I am giving you some information that could be valuable. Now, we do not have much time and as far as I can see, the pad in your hand is empty with nothing. Here is something. Now, take the breadcrumbs and follow them because I didn't just start working for Bruce yesterday, nor did I start sleeping with him yesterday. It takes years to know the amount of information I have on that family and their sadistic son who has been a terror to my family, a terror that you have yet to catch!"

The detective swallows hard, fighting back the fact that he thought Natasha was very attractive the first time he met her, but realizes she is even more beautiful as she sits in the sunlight reading him his rights. "I'm going to go check on the fellow to see if he is awake and can give me anything.

When I come up with something, you folks will be the first to know," he says as he proceeds to the door.

Natasha looks at her family and apologizes for what they just heard. The truth at this point is the truth, and now everyone is reaping the consequences of the bed she made. "If I could, I would tie that little bastard to a chair and strap steaks to his naked flesh and let hungry Rottweilers have a feast."

Bernadean smiles and puts her hands over Natasha's and says, "Vengeance is the Lord's. No one can punish or reward anyone better than God. You have to maintain your safety, protect yourself, but do not live in fear. God will take care of that disturbed child in His way in His time. You watch."

Natasha informs the family about the news on her release. She gives them special, detailed information about how she plans to go and get Landry back. Persistent about going alone, she tells everyone what she is going to do, who she has to see to get it done, and how she plans to accomplish her rescue.

Michelle says she will get her a bag and its contents will have everything she needs for this type of job. She worries for her daughter, but knowing the person Natasha is, once her mind is made, there is no stopping her.

CHAPTER THIRTY-SEVEN

A few floors away, Jeffery is feeling a tingling sensation all over his body. He has the feeling that his limbs have fallen asleep and that they are getting their feeling back, which brings a feeling of jubilee. Jeffery wants to run, but the stints won't let him.

Jeffery can wiggle his toes first. He tries flexing his calves next and they respond. He then flexes his thighs and buttocks and they reflex to his thought. Jeffery moves his fingers and presses the nurse's button on his bed rail. It takes her a moment to arrive. She thought someone was visiting him and pressed the button by accident. Not the case this time! He could press it himself. When she enters the room, Jeffery is moving his head from side to side and his body is trembling. As soon as she enters, she runs back out and gets the doctor.

Tears are running down his face because he is so happy, so excited, that for the first time in months he has feeling and it is not pain. He praises God in his cast and moans with the utterance of thanks. The doctor comes in and is shocked beyond belief because no one really thought Jeffery had a fighting chance. All the signs pointed nowhere but where he was lying in a vegetative state.

Checking his vitals and seeing that everything is good, the doctor informs him that they need to run some tests. He will need to hold still long enough for them to be done and Jeffery happily agrees. The doctor cuts the bandages from his head and Jeffery commands, "Get Natasha Billingsworth and my mother, Bernadean Pattman. They are probably in Natasha's room. She is a patient here."

Hearing his own voice is surprising. He had almost forgotten his personal sound. He had almost forgotten how the vibrations of his own words exiting his mouth made him feel alive. Being able to talk back to those who are talking is something he will never take for granted again. Life, as a whole, he vows never to take for granted again.

Two hours pass and Jeffery is tired of being poked, pricked, turned, and scanned. They are in the elevator on the way back to his room and he is deep in thought. He is excited about seeing everyone. Jeffery even thinks about going back to work, better yet, traveling. He has only been out of the country once, and he wants to stamp his passport at least ten times before he turns forty. He will have to travel annually, which is just enough for him. *I wonder, would Natasha come with me?* he asks himself silently.

As soon as he can complete his daydream, he hears a voice saying, "Be joyous, for I have given you joy. Do as I ask and tell what I commanded you and all will be well with you. I will give you your desires. All I ask is that you are obedient."

"Okay," Jeffery says. The nurse pushing him in the wheelchair asks if he is okay. He replies, "I am alive and active. I am better than okay. I am blessed."

The pair continues to his room where the door is wide open and he can hear the familiar voice that he has wished he could communicate with for the past few months. As they enter, he sees his mother first. She praises God and says, "I had no doubt you would make a full recovery. God has never let me down nor have my prayers gone unanswered. Thank You, Jesus!"

They hold an embrace for several moments as they both begin to cry tears of joy. The nurse departs after his mother's embrace, giving them their moment. Michelle and Melvin are there to greet him, as well. Michelle is delighted that she finally gets a chance to meet the guy who knocked her only daughter off her feet. "It is such a pleasure to finally meet you. I am Michelle, Natasha's mother. You already know Melvin."

Michelle steps aside and Melvin leans down to hug the fellow that has eaten at his restaurant for as long as he can remember. Melvin sighs, "I am glad you are alright, because I do not know who else in the world would put up with Natasha." They both laugh and Jeffery continues into the room.

He wheels himself a little further past everyone and sees the greatest sight of all. Natasha is sitting on his bed as radiant as she has ever looked. The sun shining on her back from the window makes her glow so angelic. Their eyes meet and immediately she is on her feet and in his lap hugging him and kissing his face. When their lips meet they feel like distant lovers. Everything else fades away in that moment. They are alone, at peace, and entranced with one another. Both of them know they could hold each other forever, and they will, if time permits.

It is like everyone left on cue, because they are the only two left in the room and the door is closed. "I have some things to tell you," Jeffery says. Natasha gets up from his lap and sits in a chair next to his bed, thinking that he will lie down. Instead, Jeffery rises from the wheelchair and begins to pace the floor in an anxious way that makes Natasha very nervous.

"When I was in the coma I could hear everything that was said around me. I knew everything that was going on. I knew every visitor that came. Everything the doctors told my mother, I heard. Everything you told me, I heard. There was one encounter I couldn't believe. God came to visit me. Not only did He visit me, but He allowed me to see this day and feel the feelings I have right now."

Jeffery is hesitant to continue. What he has to say is hard and it could get him committed to the psyche ward of the hospital. He takes a deep breath and continues, saying, "There were conditions upon His visit. A purpose for Him being at my bedside. He wanted me to inform people about some things that have been happening and are going to happen. Why? I have no idea."

He continues to pace the floor, trying to find the words to tell Natasha what he is supposed to say. It is a hard thing to tell someone that their unborn child will die and not give a full reason why. He begins to bite his lip.

Natasha sees his dismay and states, "I am sure the news will be a surprise, but the information is to help the people, not hurt them. I have had my share of conversations with God, as well. This is very new to me, too, because I wasn't a believer in the spiritual or anything of the like. Today, that is different."

Jeffery swallows hard and informs her, "God told me He is going to keep your baby. He said that you will have children with your husband, but the child that is growing in you will not fulfill its destiny at this present time, so He is going to keep him."

"That is some news. I never thought I would be the mothering type. Since it is here and I needed to deal, so far it hasn't been so bad. Seeing everything that is going on right now and the mess I have made, I truly understand the reasoning," responds Natasha.

Jeffery is looking Natasha directly in her eyes. She notices that he has lost a few pounds, but figures that is natural, considering he hasn't moved in months. His eyes pierce her soul. She wants to turn away, but she can't. Natasha is so captivated by the hazel hue of his eyes that she dares not look in any other direction.

Jeffery begins, "He also told me that you are my wife." There is a pause and then Jeffery asks, "How do you feel about that?"

Stunned by the words that just proceeded out of Jeffery's mouth Natasha begins to blush. Yes, she had hoped he would recover and had even dreamed of them being together, but with all the recent events, marriage hasn't really been in her mind. There is a long moment of silence before she speaks.

They stare into each other's eyes as Jeffery waits on a response to his question. Natasha swallows hard as a vision of their lives together dances through her mind. She begins to feel excitement and says, "I feel that I can be your wife. Do you really want to spend your life with a wreck like me? That is the question we should ask."

"I agree to forever as long as you're in agreement with me," he replies.

"For the rest of our lives it is."

CHAPTER THIRTY-EIGHT

All of the commotion has Michelle's nerves on edge. Someone has tried to kill her daughter for the second time, and come very close to succeeding again. Landry has been abducted. No one knows where she is, and time is mounting, which means she is less likely to be found alive. She has grown accustomed to her new family and Tessa being a shoulder she can rely on. Today, however, she feels enough is enough. She is going to march herself right down to the detective's office to see what is the hold-up, and what she can do to help capture the man responsible.

Hiring two bodyguards didn't do any good, so she has taken it upon herself to practice shooting in her backyard. Bryant would have target practice when home from traveling, but she didn't join him very often. With her past affecting her child the way it has, she feels a deeper need to protect her now since she didn't do so previously.

Michelle is a southern belle, so there are two guns that are popular for women living in the back woods – a trusty .22-caliber pistol to keep in her purse, and the double-barrel shot gun to carry from the truck to the house when traveling those dirt roads. After firing rounds from both weapons, Michelle wipes her brow with a linen handkerchief, pushes her Chanel sunglasses onto the bridge of her nose and heads back toward the house so she can get ready to go into the city.

Easy attire is called for with the weather as warm as it is. The periwinkle espadrilles, periwinkle seersucker walking shorts, sleeveless white poplin button-down, and a white linen blazer make Michelle look overdressed for a precinct drop-in.

The officer at the desk looks her from head to toe before he asks if he can be of any assistance. Michelle removes her glasses and asks, "May I have a word with a Detective Robert Allen? He is working the Billingsworth case. Tell him Michelle Billingsworth is here to see him."

The officer gives her a smile and is a little more polite after hearing her name. He picks up the phone on the desk and calls for Detective Allen. There is an exchange of words, but Michelle can only get one side. The officer hangs the receiver onto the base and says, "He will be right out to get you, Mrs. Billingsworth. You can have a seat there. May I get you some coffee?"

"No, thank you, kind sir. I will just wait."

Fifteen minutes go by and there is no sign of Detective Allen. Michelle is a very patient person when it comes to getting what she wants, but this matter is urgent. She checks her watch again and it has been eighteen minutes since she sat down. She approaches the clerk again, but as she is doing so he picks up the phone. By the time she reaches him, he is speaking with someone, or he appears to be. Michelle patiently waits until his conversation is finished and then asks, "How much longer is he going to be? I have been waiting for fifteen minutes. Does he need me to come back later?"

"No, ma'am. That was him on the phone. He said it is only going to be a few minutes more."

As the officer is speaking Detective Allen is coming into the precinct with another officer. He has a stack of papers in one hand and a cup of coffee in the other. There is a look of surprise on his face when he and Michelle make eye contact. He approaches her, shifts the stack of papers to his left hand with the coffee and extends the right to Michelle.

"I wasn't expecting to see you here. Is there something I can help you with?" asks the detective, not knowing she's been waiting.

"Yes, the officer here at the desk called you almost thirty minutes ago to let you know I was waiting to talk to you. Why are you surprised to see me?"

Detective Allen looks at the officer with disgust and says, "We will talk about the mix-up later." He looks back at Michelle and says, "Follow me to my office."

The three are passing the officer at the desk and only Michelle overhears something he mumbles to himself. She stops dead in her tracks and asks, "Do you want to say that a little louder?"

The other officer and Detective Allen stop and look at each other, because they hadn't heard anything. The officer on the other side of the counter bites hard before repeating what he previously stated. Michelle moves closer to the counter, both feet planted, and faces the officer directly. She looks over her glasses then asks, "Could you please repeat what you said? I don't think I heard you clearly."

When the officer stands grudgingly and leans in her direction, Michelle doesn't flinch, shift, or bat an eyelash. He looks her in the face as if she is an old dish rag and says, "High-society house nigger. You can wait as long as it takes." Before she knows it, Michelle reacts. All of the fear, anger, and hurt that she experienced living in the back woods of Mississippi have found her in New York City. She slaps the officer with all she has. Detective Allen appears between the two as the officer rubs his jaw. Michelle loses weight in all the stress so she isn't surprised to see her four-carat wedding set has found its way to the inside of her hand. The officer has a cut about half an inch long, but nothing too severe.

"I'm going to have to arrest you, Michelle, for assaulting an officer," informs Detective Allen. He begins to Mirandize her and takes his cuffs from their holster. The officer that was assaulted says, "Don't lock her up. It didn't happen if she's willing to accept my apology."

Michelle places her sun wear in her purse while Detective Allen still has a good grip on her bicep. She looks the officer she assaulted in the eye and says, "Every person that walks past you is your neighbor. You are to love your neighbor so that Christ can love you. Now, I had no business retaliating and going 'cross ya face. For that I am sorry, and yes, I accept your apology, as well."

Michelle continues with her speech, saying, "Do you know true black history? It's because of blacks that there is sanitation, civilization, and animal domestication. We have been inventing and creating things going back six thousand years. Take your family to the museum and look at the art. Tell me the color of the face of those great people. It will change your mind and your heart."

She walks over and shakes his hand. They share a smile and go their separate ways.

When the three arrive at the detective's office there is paper everywhere, along with empty coffee cups and newspapers. Michelle is surprised and even a little disgusted. "Isn't there someone from the city that can come and clean the offices? It looks like dis job is too big for just you," she states.

Detective Allen just laughs and clears a chair for her to sit. The other officer just takes a seat on a pile of papers on an adjacent desk, while Allen sits behind the one with the most papers. "We have had several detectives who have been arrested for various crimes. Therefore, my workload has exploded and they are working on getting me some help. The assistance can't get here fast enough, I'm afraid," states Detective Allen.

"Where does that leave my daughter? This is the second time someone has tried to kill her and there hasn't been an arrest. She is getting out of the hospital and I need to know that crazy person has been put away. Not to mention Landry has been kidnapped!" says Michelle with a look of concern on her face.

Detective Allen looks defeated when he says, "I'm doing all I can to find the guy she named, but I can't catch him to question him."

"I hired security but they were no good. My family believes in bearing arms, Detective and that's what got Jeffery crossed in all this. We need action taken now before someone else gets hurt. I would hate for this situation to turn into a homicide investigation. This officer over here looks able-bodied. Get him to do some work and not just looking in my mouth," commands Michelle.

"Detective, could you leave us a moment please?" asks Detective Allen. He waits until the officer can't be heard going down the hallway before he asks Michelle questions. He begins by asking, "Mrs. Billingsworth, is there anything that has struck you as unusual since Natasha has been in the hospital, or even the events leading up to it?"

"Well, Detective, my daughter and I haven't been close, so anything strange wouldn't be recognized by me. Although we did meet her siblings by another woman, and that was strange and unusual by itself," Michelle states.

"Do you have any reason to believe that they could have any connection to anything?"

"Not that I can see. We have gotten along wonderfully so far. What are you implying, Detective?" Michelle asks, leaning forward in her seat, closer to him.

"Mrs. Billingsworth, I just want you to look at it from my point of view. They have motive. Jealous siblings, the mistress, these things must be taken into account in these cases. You could even be considered in the matter. Your husband is deceased. You fired the maid, so there is no one to account for your whereabouts. Maybe it was you who drove to your daughter's house and caused all this mayhem," says Detective Allen. At this point he is leaning back in his chair. The look in his eyes makes it seem as if he is watching the story of a movie unfold. Too bad the movie has Michelle pegged as the villain.

Michelle gets her items together so that she can leave the office. Before she walks out of the door she turns back and looks at Detective Allen. Michelle starts by saying, "Do you really think I would harm my own child, my flesh and blood?" She shakes her head, puts on her glasses, and begins to give her closing remarks. "I hate it when people have nothing to do but make up stories. I'm not your man, Detective, and if I was, I have the means to get the job done right, and to get the hell out of here. Also, she is all I have left. I didn't come to see you just to slap around your officers and be accused of something I didn't do. Let me know when you decide to get off your ass and do some real cops' work. Otherwise, we will get it done ourselves. "

Michelle exits the office with the same elegant stride she had entered with. The officer she assaulted is still at the counter. He smiles and tells her to have a nice day. Michelle stops, turns on her heels and approaches the desk. She asks the officer, "Do you have family?"

He replied, "Yes, a wife and two children."

"I'm not going to get into your business, but I know there is one thing that can stress a husband out — lack of money." As Michelle is saying this, she places her purse on the counter, pulls out her wallet and begins writing a check. She hands over the piece of paper worth twenty thousand dollars and says, "Happy wife, happy life. At least you can relax for a while and enjoy them. You never know when you will never see them again."

"I can't take that."

"Do not be so prideful. It is going to clear, trust me. You be blessed, and I suggest you write your name in the blank otherwise someone else will get the fortune because I'm leaving it right on this counter."

Michelle walks away and feels a little better than she did before she entered the building. Detective Allen has some nerve accusing her and suggesting the family had something to do with everything with his line of questioning. It looks like Michelle will have to do what she knows to do.

Cops don't always get their man, so a private eye would be the perfect help in this situation. She knows just who to call. It is unfortunate that the case will be closed before he can even get started.

CHAPTER THIRTY-NINE

It is a strange request for Natasha to ask everyone to go about their business and not make a big fuss about her getting out of the hospital. The doctor sees no reason for Jeffery to stay, so he is released the same Thursday as his future wife.

Wig, heavy makeup, and glasses disguise Natasha and make her look a little crazy. Jeffery holds the humor of her appearance to himself until they are in the car and sure no one is following them.

The two of them realize how long they were inside and take in the scenery of the city. The colors, people speed-walking, and the smell of the restaurants have them hypnotized. All of a sudden Natasha makes a request, "Could we stop to get a burger?"

Jeffery laughs and answers, "Whatever you want. It's yours."

"Afterward, we are going to make a stop at Bruce Wilson's place. I have to get my cousin back and stop this once and for all."

Jeffery knows Natasha isn't the type to sit around and let things happen. He doesn't like that he will be the one to take her to her ex-lover's house, but he is grateful they have a closeness that holds no judgment.

"Are you sure that is a good idea? Remember you are pregnant and getting too stressed can land you back in the hospital," Jeffery asks.

"My cousin is dying by the minute and I can't just let a psycho take his anger out on her just to get to me."

They stop by the nearby grill and have a bite to eat before embarking on the trip that will not only change their day, but their lives.

***

It is not a surprise that Bruce still has his burner phone that hardly anyone knows about. Natasha isn't a fool to think she had been the only woman, or the only reason he still had the phone.

After two rings Bruce answers, "Natasha?"

"We are coming up to your door right now. Good thing the door man knew me from the news. We have to talk."

Bruce pauses before replying to her statement. He is alone and makes a note that she had said 'We'. Natasha is a classy woman, but with everything that has happened, he can only hope that trait is still intact.

It only takes Bruce a few seconds before answering the door. He looks tired, hopeless, and pale. Moving to the side, he lets the couple into the penthouse he shares with his wife, his children, and the help.

Natasha is too uncomfortable to go deep into the house, knowing who lives there. All she has is one question. She needs to ask it face-to-face so that she can make sure Bruce isn't lying.

"Where is your dock on the harbor? I know your son is keeping my cousin there. Tell me," Natasha demands.

Bruce shakes his head, rubs his pale face and says, "He was spiraling out of control even before the news of my infidelity. That just sent him over the edge. For what it's worth, I'm sorry."

Natasha looks Bruce in the face and says, "I apologize for my part in our affair. A family was what I wanted, yet my actions wrecked yours. I hate that I was the straw that broke the camel's back."

"Dock thirty-seven is where the boat is. There is a little station right off the drive that is used to house equipment. How do you know she is there?" Bruce asks, as if he never thought that might be where his son would hide.

"A dream. Thanks for your help, and I am truly sorry for all of this."

The duo exits the penthouse and Jeffery feels that it wasn't as bad as it could have been. He has a new respect for Natasha. Being pregnant and facing the father after all the happenings would stress any other woman beyond belief. Jeffery is curious about why she didn't inform Bruce of the pregnancy. "Why didn't you tell him about the baby?" Jeffery asks.

"He knows. There is nothing left to say to him. After we get my cousin back, never talking to him or seeing that family again will be fine by me. We need to get Landry back today. My mother packed what we would need in my bag."

When they get back into the vehicle, it is approaching dusk on the Upper East Side. It will take thirty minutes for the two to get there and it will be dark when they do. Jeffery wants a plan. He is fresh off a stretcher, cast, and bandages and isn't excited to be put into a situation that could land him in a coffin this time.

CHAPTER FORTY

Natasha is focused but afraid of the outcome. The past few days have been overwhelming but she can only think about how her actions got her cousin in harm's way. She is tired and pregnant and has had enough of all the drama. Natasha pulls the bag into her lap from the floor beneath her in the car and unzips it to view its contents.

Michelle must have had a checklist when packing the bag. There is a change of clothes, towels, a 9mm, a pocketknife, a lock-picking kit, a flashlight, gel pepper spray, and a large baton. Natasha pulls the gun out and immediately Jeffery becomes uneasy.

Jeffery asks, "Do you think we really need that? I don't want a repeat of history."

"I'm putting it in the glove box. There is a baton, pocketknife, and flashlight I figure you could use. I will take the pepper spray and pick the lock. Hopefully, they will just have her tied up so we can get in and you help her out."

They pull the car into the drive just before dock thirty-seven. The breeze is cool against their face as they step out of the car. They meet at the trunk and embrace like lovers who have been kept apart by war. Both are dressed in jeans, black tees and sneakers. With their weapons in possession, they walk toward the dock hand-in-hand.

As they draw closer, the little building comes into view. There is only one light on in one of the rooms on the top floor of the two story building. There are slit windows along the bottom that implies there is a basement to this brick building.

Jeffery pulls Natasha to him and holds her close once again, saying, "This is the beginning of our lives together. We are coming out alive, unharmed, and with Landry. Stay as low as possible and stay behind me. I love you, Natasha, even though you shot me."

They surprisingly chuckle at the joke and she replies, "I love you, too."

They trot toward the building believing they are undetected. Shining the light into the basement they cannot see if Landry is inside because the windows are blackened. They know then they have the right place. Running around to the back, they approach the door. Jeffery checks it and it is locked. Natasha picks the lock. It takes her a few minutes to get it open. This puts Jeffery's mind at ease because if she had been able to open it easily there would be a little more sharing that needs to be done on Natasha's part.

Entering the building, they notice it has the dank and musty smell of a place that has been sitting uninhabited for some time. The light from the upstairs beams to their right, revealing a staircase that leads to the second floor. There is fishing equipment along the walls ascending as the stairs do, as if it were art.

The same light illuminates the main floor dimly to show a work desk that is empty, a large old sofa, and a few random chairs spread about the area in no particular order. The front door is directly in front of the back door on the other side of the building with a large window behind the empty desk to the left of the door.

There is an even darker corner to the right of the main entrance. This leads Natasha to believe that this is where the stairs leading to the basement would be. As far as they can tell, there is no separate exit from the basement. They will have to go down and back out again the same way they entered. Closing the door behind them, they make their way to the darkest part of the place without using their flashlight. Someone will know something is wrong if there is a light on upstairs and a flashlight shining in another level of the building.

The two of them make it to the door without disturbing anything. They look at each other and take a breath. "Here we go. Brace yourself and be careful. I need for you to stay as close to the bottom of the stairs as possible to be the lookout," Jeffery orders.

He turns the knob. It lets out this eerie screech that wails from being old and unused. They hear movement that is faint and could be a rodent. They proceed down the stairs hand-in-hand.

When they reach the bottom, Natasha turns on the flashlight. She held the light at eye level in her left hand and slowly flashes the room, starting to her left. There is a window that is blackened like the rest, but it is larger than the slits on the other side. The room is noticeably clean with only cobwebs and the scent of body odor. As Natasha continues to shine the light going clockwise, she hears some movement again.

"Landry," she says in a loud whisper. Moans come soon after she calls Landry's name. Natasha shines the light in that direction and there is her cousin. Landry is a horrific sight, due to her having been down there for days. On her, there are rat feces and scratch and bite marks, and she is sitting in her own waste.

Natasha begins to run to her, but Jeffery stops her by putting his arm up. He looks Natasha in the face and says, "You are to look out and listen to make sure no one sneaks up on us." She nods to show she understands and places both shaking hands on the flashlight.

Jeffery gets over to Landry in a flash with the pocketknife in hand, ready to go to work on the duct tape that has her restrained. He starts sawing at the tape on her ankles. Landry's smell engulfs his personal space and makes him a little nauseous. This is a rescue mission. He had had certain expectations of what she would look like after being in a basement for a few days, but he wasn't prepared for this. No one could prepare for this.

The sound of freedom is promising when the knife goes through the tape around the ankles. As Jeffery starts on the hands, Natasha whispers loudly, "Hurry! I think I hear someone upstairs."

He starts digging faster and applying more pressure. Someone had placed more tape around the wrists, making it more difficult to cut.

Suddenly a light comes on and the door to the entrance swings open. Natasha is frightened to the point that she drops the flashlight. Jeffery continues to cut. One more millimeter and Landry will be free. The sweat from his brow begins to drip from his nose. Landry is crying with her lips together, trying to mute the sound.

Natasha hops into the little nook in front of the window to the left of the stairs. Cobwebs entangle themselves around her head but she manages not to scream. She hears the thump of footsteps coming into the basement. She prays that they will be unseen, Landry and Jeffery will be out of sight, and that they will get out of this alive.

A snap of the tape is the sound of freedom Landry has longed for since her capture. With the footsteps getting louder the two scurry underneath the steps. As they crouch there, Landry hides behind Jeffery as best she can, and no matter the effort, she can't be as silent as she would like. Overwhelming is this experience and she will only be able to relax when it is over.

Thump, thump, thump, comes the sound of the boots taking the last three steps. The grind of shoes turning on their heels lets them know the guilty is on their level, and has the upper hand because he knows where they are, and they have nowhere to run.

EPILOGUE

Standing under the light of the basement is Bruce's son. He is armed with a .45 in his belt but nothing in his hands. Arrogant in his thinking, he doesn't care he is outnumbered, but feels as if he has them right where he wants them.

Behind the cases under the stairs are Landry and Jeffery. He is calculating what to do next in his mind. He only sees but the shadow of the abductor.

"I have nowhere to go, and nothing I would rather be doing than killing you three. You can come out now and get it over with, or wait and I will kill you slowly," summons Bruce's son.

Jeffery begins to pray. Landry's tears begin to show dampness on the back of his shirt. He knows he has to do something. Jeffery turns to Landry and places his finger over his lips, telling her to be quiet. He peeks out from behind the crates and soon stands facing their attacker. He is thinking about their first encounter months prior and how it led to his near-death experience.

"We meet again! So brave of you to stick around. So brave of you to defend your whore. Or so you may think; it is not bravery at all, but stupidity. And you will be buried with 'Stupid Lover' on your tombstone."

Jeffery swallows hard, pretending not to see Natasha in the shadow by the window. Bruce's son didn't pick up the flashlight she had dropped. It lies there still on and illuminating their feet. Jeffery puts his hands up and is trying to find the words that will talk down this crazed man.

Jeffery begins by saying, "I can't imagine what you feel that would drive you to a measure such as this. I am a lawyer and you are heaping charges on your head that will put you away for a long time."

"I'm not going to jail!"

"What do you believe your fate will be after all of this?" Jeffery asks.

"Fate! I create my own fate. What I do is the creation of my mind and I am free mentally and therefore will never be jailed." Pulling the gun from the holster and aiming it at Jeffery, he prepares to pull the trigger. "Shall we pray?"

Jeffery is afraid that this is the day he will die. He looks back over the past few days in his mind and thinks about what God charged him to say to those he knew. He is on a mission to complete that task. Natasha knows what is to come in the near future for her child, but she is only one person on his agenda. "What about what you told me to do, God?"

Just as the question enters Jeffery's thoughts, he can see the movement of the flashlight's beam. Behind Bruce's son is Natasha coming full force with the flashlight over her head, ready to attack. Her teeth are clenched and there is a rage in her eyes that lets Jeffery know the blow could be fatal. There is a cracking sound when the flashlight and Bruce Junior's head make contact.

The next few moments move in slow motion as the gun falls from his hands. His eyes roll back in his head as he falls to his knees. Natasha still has the flashlight in hand and is ready to strike again if he makes any movement. His lifeless body hits the floor. Not another sound. Not another word.

Jeffery kicks the gun away. Kneeling down to check his pulse, he says, "It is very faint. Get Landry and let's go. I will call the police when we get to the car."

Natasha goes to retrieve Landry, who is still hiding under the stairs with her head on her knees. She has the appearance of a scared child. Landry touches Natasha's face and says, "I want to go home."

Made in the USA
Columbia, SC
15 March 2021